Tim's Place

written and illustrated

by

Judith I. Fringuello

NU LEAF
PUBLISHING
Emerson, New Jersey

NU⌀LEAF PUBLISHING

15 Orchard Avenue
Emerson, New Jersey 07630

Printed in the United States of America

Library of Congress Catalog Card Number:
97-91958

Page 153 from THE PROPHET by Kahlil Gibran
Copyright 1923 by Kahlil Gibran and renewed
1951 by administrators CTA of Kahlil Gibran
Estate and Mary G. Gibran.
Reprinted by permission of Alfred A. Knopf, Inc.

Cover: Photography by Romildo Fringuello
Technical Support by Lisa Kennedy

Some names of persons and places have been changed
to protect the privacy of those involved

Dedication

$\mathcal{J}$ dedicate this true story to every mother who has watched helplessly her child suffer in pain.

Trust your instincts! You know your child better than anyone. For your child's sake, be a squeaky wheel even if it means making a fool of yourself. Make waves! You're dealing with people who are human just like you and me. They get distracted. They make mistakes. They have their own agenda. Remember, medicine is more of an art than a science.

And although God seems far away, take heart. He is there by your side. Call on him for comfort.

You are not alone.

Judith Fringuello

Contents

Acknowledgements

$\mathcal{G}$ would like to thank those people who have given me help and encouragement while writing this book:

Sharon Spencer, English professor at Montclair State College;

Amy Sunshine, Rheta Sellittti and the late Betsy Scanlan for editing and proofreading;

Fred Canavan and Catherine Egan for allowing me to use their words of comfort;

Marisa Roscio, my sister-in-law, who never lost faith in my ability to write this;

And my husband, Ronnie, who stood by me during this time of trial.

Preface

*A*s I look over what I have written the issues which loomed so large and dramatic at the time now seem trivial by comparison to the medical breakthroughs of today. The field of transplantation has opened up to a degree unthinkable 30 years ago. New drugs have made the impossible, possible. Cloning and all its moral ramifications is on the horizon.

Attitudes have changed drastically. In my mother's day all the doctor wanted to know was the state of his patient's bowels. In the 50's the doctor was placed on a pedestal. The patient was not expected to have an opinion. Now there is such an explosion of information due to the internet that patients are becoming informed consumers. The doctor is prepared to be questioned and is expected to listen to the patient's concerns.

I only pray that my son's ordeal played a role, no matter how small, in the grand scheme of things and that a person facing these new medical challenges will be better prepared to take charge of his own destiny.

1

This time it will be different

I strain to open the huge steel door. Its hinges are well oiled and once started it moves easily. More like a door to a prison than a hospital, I muse, as it closes heavily behind me.

I walk briskly along the hall. As I pass the cafeteria, two men are busily putting up a sign, CAUTION! WET FLOOR. The pungent odor of ammonia pierces my nostrils. No hint of the food inside. How different from Wakefield Hospital. There, the aroma of cooked cabbage lingered like the inside of a stale tenement.

I wait for the elevator as people bustle about, some with white jackets, some with obvious infirmities. You never know, you might be standing next to a world renowned surgeon or the poorest derelict in New York City, I speculate as I ride four flights up to dialysis.

I step out into a marble-floored vestibule. It's clean and well lighted. Not like Wakefield at all. I walk timidly down the hall. Will he be poked full of tubes with bottles dripping? This time I won't be shocked. I'll prepare for the worst. I guess the worst was when he was a month old. He was strapped down in the crib. There was even a tube into the soft spot in his head. He could only make a mewing sound like a kitten.

I glance quickly into the first room. That isn't him, or is it? Oh, yes, I forgot, he has a little moustache now. I try to enter noiselessly, afraid to disturb him or his roommate.

"Hi Mom, what's new?" He's awake and alert. I can't believe

he had surgery only yesterday.

An intern and floor nurse enter to change his dressing and check the drainage. They are efficient and pleasant.

The nurse carries in a sterilized package carefully wrapped.

"What surprise do you have for me this time?" Tim asks wryly.

"Oh, just a needle." She casually glances at him from the corner of her eye. It occurs to me she might be flirting.

"Where is it going?"

"Where do you think?" she jokes softly.

"Oh, no," he groans in mock agony. "I've had about eight there already. I'll be a Swiss cheese."

"Excuse me," she says as she sweeps the curtain around the bed. Oh, yes. I forgot. He's a man now. I'm excluded from such intimate things. I choke back the desire to laugh.

I'm envious the way he handles pain so well. Better than I can. He has earned his place of respect among the nursing staff. He never seems to complain except for the food. Today is no exception.

"I haven't had anything to eat for two days."

"No lunch?"

"Well, if you call some chicken fat floating around in a bowl of hot water, lunch. I mean FOOD."

A stocky, gray-haired man purposefully enters the room. I struggle to recognize him. Is it Dr. Brody? Yes, it must be. Funny, I pictured him heavier. He stretches out his hand.

"It's been a long time since we've seen each other." He tries to be friendly but there is something impersonal about his handshake. "How have you been?"

"Fine," I stammer. Why do I always clam up when I have a million questions to ask?

He talks briefly to Tim and seems satisfied.

"Have they fed you yet? Well, you'll be getting dinner. You did fine, yesterday, Tim, just fine." He turns and is gone.

A minute-and-a-half exam. Fifty dollars probably or more, I calculate.

Tim snickers. "I did well? All I did was lie there like a sack of potatoes."

"He means you responded well to the anesthesia. You know, your blood pressure stayed down. You didn't give them any problems."

"Yeah."

The food tray comes and he wolfs down the roast chicken.

"Don't eat so fast. You'll get gas."

"Tomorrow, bring me some Macintosh apples and some chocolate bars."

I check his diet sheet. Eating is going to be a problem. No salt or sodium, no cheese, no prepared cakes or pastry containing baking soda, limited fluids. Cut back on fruits, especially bananas. Meat, one serving a day. Unsalted bread and butter. People don't realize how boring rice and noodles get over a long period of time. Living on dialysis is no picnic. Last time I ate all the things he wasn't suppose to eat, and look at me. Not this time. This time it will be different.

I say goodbye and kiss him on the top of his head. He's not embarrassed. "I'm glad you came." The quiet way he says this brings a wave of the old guilt flooding over me. I should have been here before.

"I won't be here tomorrow but probably on the weekend."

"Okay"

I leave quickly, putting on my coat by the elevator. It whines to a stop and I squeeze into its crowed interior. It hadn't been as bad as I had expected. Maybe those bad times were only a figment of my imagination. Maybe last time it was worse because he was so young and I was trying to live it for him.

The steel door bangs behind me. The frosty February air clears the stuffiness from my head. It feels good to be outside. The coldness sharpens and stirs my memories of those bad times. As I walk to the subway, I remember other trips over the same route. Tim's whole life can be defined by hospital episodes, as if he had been singled out from the beginning. But why?

There was nothing unusual about my pregnancy or Tim's birth. I nursed him just as I had nursed his brother, Leo. He was born one day before his father's birthday, October 28, 1956.

We had been home about a month when Leo began to run a high fever. I called Dr. Lawrence. He'd delivered Timmy, and I had especially chosen him because he was an old fashioned doctor who would care for the whole family. And, he made house-calls.

Dr. Lawrence examined Leo, who was 17 months old, and put him on penicillin. He also examined Timmy who, judging by the fullness of my breasts, was off his regular amount of milk. The doctor found nothing out of the ordinary and prescribed nothing.

Leo took all my time. He was a demanding child when well and now wanted to be held and rocked constantly. I was thankful the baby was not fussing. I wrapped Timmy tightly in a receiving blanket and placed him tenderly in the bassinette.

That night Leo's temperature went up to 105 degrees. Aspirin didn't help. I tried to bring the fever down by bathing him with cool water, but that made him scream, which in turn kept his fever up.

The next day the doctor examined Leo again.

"You have to give the medicine time to work," he reassured me. "Keep giving him aspirin and sponge baths."

"What about the baby?" I asked, hiding my anxious feelings. Deep down I knew something was not right. My breasts were full and leaking. Timmy had slept through the night and his diaper was hardly damp. This was unusual for a newborn but I was still new at this and too timid to assert myself.

"I don't know what to tell you," said Dr. Lawrence shaking down the thermometer. "His temperature is *below* normal."

I was beginning to get scared and a little angry. "Suppose I call in someone else, a specialist?"

"That's up to you." Dr. Lawrence sounded a little unsure of himself. He didn't offer any other advice as he hastily packed up his bag and left.

The seriousness of the situation began to sink in. Who should I call? What was the name of the pediatric group in Englewood, the one my friend bragged about? Think! Try to concentrate! Was it Hillman? That's it. Hillman and Juliano. I found the number and dialed the phone. A busy signal. That figures, with a reputation like theirs. I hung up and tried again. Still busy. The minutes slipped by. Again. Leo called crankily from his crib. At last the line was ringing. The switchboard answered.

"I need a doctor right away. My 17 month old son has a temperature of 105 and the baby...he...he's not taking anything by mouth...I don't think."

The receptionist was not very sympathetic. After all, my children were not regular patients. She had never heard of me and I must have sounded vague and incoherent. The doctor, she said, would be at my house... later.

I paced up and down, Leo on my hip, the baby in the crook of my arm. I lost track of time. Should I call again? It must have been hours. I offered the baby water. He refused to take it. His cry frightened me. Such a helpless wail. Oh hell, I'm going to call again. So what if they think I'm a hysterical mother. It's my children who are important.

This time she knew my voice. "The doctor is making other calls. He's had a busy day. Don't worry. He'll be there."

"I'm sorry, but tell him to please hurry. They're both very sick." I took a deep breath and tried to control myself. Looking back, I should have bundled them up and gone to the emergency room of the hospital. But, I wasn't aware how serious the situation really was.

About 5 p.m. the doctor finally arrived. Leo was the first to be examined. "But the one I'm really worried about is Timmy," I said as I unwrapped the little blanket.

The doctor took the baby and examined him thoroughly. "This baby is dehydrated," he said. There was a certainty in his voice with a hint of urgency.

"Dehydrated? What does that mean?"

"We have to get him to the hospital immediately and feed him fluids intravenously. He may have an intestinal blockage. It's not unusual in newborns."

By then, my husband Ronnie, was home from work. We rushed Tim to the hospital. The next day they operated to take a look at his intestines but there was no blockage. What was causing his illness?

"You can visit for ten minutes," said the business-like nurse in the intensive care unit.

I walked into the room. There, in a huge metal crib was my son, no bigger than a doll, his arms and legs strapped down, tubes coming out of every part of his tiny body. How cruel it seemed. What were they doing to him? Had they no feelings? Tears came in a rush. I wanted to cuddle him in my arms but instead gently rubbed the side of his head where they had shaved it for the blood transfusion.

"Tim-Tim?" I called softly.

The corner of his mouth seemed to turn up in a silent smile. Was it only gas? No, I'm sure he recognized my voice.

"Your ten minutes are up now." Reluctantly, I surrendered him to the sterile but capable hands of the hospital staff. Half of me was relieved of the burden of responsibility briefly lifted but the other half ached because I knew I was the only one who could give him the love he needed.

At home, Leo's temperature remained high. The doctors admitted they were baffled. What could be causing this double calamity?

Dr. Juliano called. "I hate to tell you this, Mrs. Fringuello, but I feel we should bring Leo into the hospital for observation. We have to get that fever down and take some tests."

Both my children in the hospital? Leo had been separated from me only once before, when Timmy was born. Staying alone in the hospital would be a traumatic experience for him, but we had to find out what was causing the fever. I knew if it remained high too long it might cause brain damage.

It took several days for tests and several more waiting for results. Finally, the doctor called. "They both have contracted the staphylococcus germ. We want to test both you and your husband to see if one of you is the carrier."

It was me. I was the carrier. That intense chill a couple of weeks ago must have been the incubation period. While I never actually became ill, I had carried the germ and spread it to the ones I loved most. Years later, I read about the staph epidemic of the fifties. Newborn babies were exposed to "hospital staph" in nurseries that were believed to be clean and sterile. This germ was an extremely stubborn bacterium that defied most antiseptic precautions. While staph causes boils in many cases, with us it chose to spread insidiously from within. This was to be Tim's first brush with death.

Once the correct medication was determined, Leo's fever subsided, Tim recovered from the surgery and things returned to normal...for the children. Tim's sudden weaning left me with engorged breasts. The doctor gave me pills to dry up my ample milk supply but they hardly helped at all. I found sleeping difficult and was miserable for weeks.

Tim's first hospital incident frightened me. It reminded me of my brother Richard. I was eight when he contracted spinal meningitis and died at one year. His death changed the direction of my mother's life. She went out to work to try to cover up the pain. Why had Tim been spared and Richard allowed to die? My mother had prayed for her son's death when she heard he probably would be mentally retarded if he had lived.

I thought back when I first suspected I was pregnant with Tim. I hadn't planned for the next child to come so soon. I remember praying to let the seed in me be transplanted into some sterile woman who wanted children badly. Maybe God was punishing me for having had those thoughts. No...I don't believe God to be a vengeful God. He would never make an innocent child suffer for the sins of his parents. But if Tim had never been born, think of the pain he would have been spared.

Why do I keep remembering the bad times? There were good times, too. Tim remembers them. He was a happy child, always laughing. His father called him "Butterball".

I can still see him with his shapeless cowboy hat jammed on his head, bamboo pole in his hand, running down the hill as fast as his stubby legs would carry him, yelling. "Wait for me, you guys!"

I am jolted back to the present as the subway screeches to a halt. It is a short ride to the bridge. The crowd pushes me through the doors and up the steps. Automatically, I climb the long ramp to the upper level. The rush hour is beginning. There is a long queue at the bus stop but it moves quickly. I find a seat by the window. The lights of the city blur as we race through the winter evening.

I look out the bus window into the darkness. Winter evenings are so short. We must be almost there. Yes, we are crossing the railroad tracks. The good times slip back into oblivion. I struggle out of the cramped space and over the person next to me.

"Orchard Avenue," I call ahead to the driver. The narrow aisle is not meant for short, chubby people like me. As the bus screeches to a stop, I stumble to the front and down the steps. Home at last!

Our house. It must be at least 80 years old by now. When we bought it, eighteen years ago, the deed said, *over 60*. It was one of the first ones built on our block. I study it critically as I approach. Two tall skinny stories plus an attic. Unusual looking, it is sort of a cross between a colonial and a cape. Inside the rooms are small, especially the bedrooms, virtually no closets, stairways big enough for midgets, huge windows each a different measurement and one bathroom. It must have been built with leftover lumber by a drunken carpenter. When we bought it, I swore I would put up with it for three years at the most. Yet, we raised five children here, somehow. We could have chosen a newer house in the Continental Woods development. But those houses were even smaller with no cellar or attic and they all looked alike. At least this house had character.

I climb the bluestone steps to the front door. This part of the house was new. Ronnie and the masonry teacher from Bergen Tech completely renovated the porch section, brick-faced the front and with imaginative landscaping transformed our image from poor white to middle class.

As I opened the door Nikki barks her greeting. What a watchdog. Her German Shepherd background makes her look fierce but at heart she's a softy. Arthritis has made her back legs stiff and it takes her a few minutes to get up to meet me. I cross the living room almost falling over the body sprawled there.

"Hi, Mom." Eleven year old Amy unglues herself from the TV.

"Hi. Anybody home yet?"

"Not yet."

I take off my coat and go into the kitchen. What can I throw together fast for supper?

"Amy!" I call, my voice purposely annoyed, "Let's go! You haven't emptied the clean dishes from the dishwasher yet. And the table needs setting. It's late."

"Okay, okay, you don't have to yell."

I find some unthawed hamburger in the refrigerator and begin to make patties. It will only take ten minutes or so for rice and string beans.

"Do you want a salad?" I ask Amy. She nods. "Then help me fix it."

The back door opens and Donna clomps in. Nikki goes through her barking routine.

"Where have you been? Didn't you have to go to work?" I ask with surprise.

"Mom, that was yesterday. Don't you remember? I had a yearbook meeting tonight and I switched my hours."

"Oh, I forgot."

"I put my new schedule on the bulletin board, didn't you see it?"

"No."

The bulletin board is overflowing with calendars, school notices, odd scrapes of paper with phone numbers, Weight Watchers recipes. Mothers are supposed to remember everything. At least I don't have to pick her up from the A & P tonight at ten o'clock.

"Help me with the salad," I call futilely as she disappears up the stairs. High school seniors are in a world of their own.

A car pulls into the driveway. It's twenty-year-old Lisa. Nikki really goes wild. She thinks Lisa belongs to her.

"Hi, Nickel," Lisa coos in a high voice scratching the dog behind the ears. "Hi, Mom. How's Tim?"

"Not bad. He looks pretty good. How did things go at work?"

"You'll never guess what we photographed today. A bathtub with a live model. It was my job to keep the soap bubbles bubbling."

"In the nude?"

"Almost. From the waist up. Boy, was she skinny. And she made $100 an hour. Can you imagine?"

Lisa is enthusiastic about her job at the photo studio. I'm glad. She's finally getting a sense of direction.

"Can you cut up some tomatoes and lettuce for a salad?"

"In a minute. I have to call Susan."

I pull out the salad ingredients from the refrigerator and place them in a colander under cold running water. Ronnie walks in.

"What's cooking?" He lifts the lid to the rice letting out all the steam.

"Nothing special," I mumble closing the cover tightly.

"How's Tim?"

"I'll tell you at dinner. Right now I'm trying to get it all together."

"Was he awake?" Ronnie asks ignoring the brush-off.

"Yes. I was surprised how good he looked. Dr. Brody was pleased with him."

"You saw Brody?"

"The one and only. Here, put the bread on the table. And call the kids. It's time to eat."

Just as we are sitting down, Leo, the unpredictable one, arrives with appetite in tow. He squeezes his lanky twenty-three year old frame into the extra chair.

"You made it just in time before the vultures attack," Ronnie jokes. He likes to see the table full with his family.

"Mom, did you see Tim today?" Leo asks casually, trying not to let his concern for his younger brother show.

"Yes, he was sitting up in bed yelling for food."

Ronnie chuckles. "He must be doing okay."

"I was really surprised how well he's taking it. He's not depressed or anything. I guess dialysis isn't as bad as last time. It's a good thing they took the diseased kidney out. It was making him feel miserable."

As I gaze around the table, I notice the empty place. Ronnie catches my eye and we exchange glances. Tim's seven year hiatus is at an end. He has lived a next-to-normal life for seven years. Now we must face new decisions, search for new answers, pray for new miracles.

This time it will be different, I tell myself. We have experience. We're hardened. And Tim is a man now.

Be not afraid of life. Believe that life
is worth living, and your belief
will help create the fact.

William James
from
The Will to Believe (1897)

2

Mixing oil and vinegar

I open the back door and look out. The yard is wall-to-wall kids. Donna's high school graduation party has increased unexpectedly to include the whole class, plus others, some being complete strangers from surrounding towns.

"Ronnie," I fret, "did you see the mob of kids out there?"

"That's nothing. Look out the front window," he replies.

The front lawn is packed and overflowing into the street with bodies. A car, trying to pass down Orchard Avenue, is barely moving. Teenagers are everywhere.

"We'd better notify the police, just in case," I remark anxiously.

"I already took care of that," Ronnie retorts. "Stop worrying. It's okay. Everything is under control."

I can count on Ronnie to stay calm. He's at his best in times of crisis, thank God. He planned the party with Donna and it is running smoothly in spite of the fact there are five times the number of people they had expected.

Inside, our guests do not seem to be upset. Ronnie's friends from the business are here. His secretary is helping cook hundreds of hotdogs with sauerkraut. As fast as they pass the food out the door, it disappears.

"Why don't you see if anyone needs a drink," Ronnie calls over his shoulder as he gets out a new tray of ice cubes. He is trying to keep my mind off the crowd outside.

I meander into the living room where everyone is relaxing.

13

"When did you paint this one?" One of my guests asks me about the line drawing of the ballerina I have hanging over the sofa.

"Oh, that's not new. I did it in figure drawing class at Pratt years ago. I recently reframed it. When I put it in a local art show, it got a blue ribbon."

"It's beautiful. You're so lucky to be talented. Your paintings are all so different."

"That's my problem. I can never decide on which media or technique I should stick with. I love them all. I'm always experimenting. I don't have time to build up a real style of my own."

I try to listen to the conversation between Ronnie's business partner and Doris, Roberto's wife. Roberto does camera work for Ronnie. He is self-employed, very thin and very Italian. His passion for his work reminds me of Ronnie twenty years ago.

"You know what he has me doing now?" Doris says with a giggle. "Developing negatives."

I can't resist butting in. "What about your youngest boy? He doesn't go to school yet, does he?"

"Not yet. He brings his toys and stays at the shop while I work." Doris obviously enjoys sharing the work load of the business with her husband. Just like Ronnie and I use to do, I think to myself. I use to keep Amy in her playpen right in the office. She cut her teeth on the phone cord. I did the payroll between diaper changes.

Doris's conversation continues as she describes how her family works and plays together. It sounds convincing but a little too optimistic. I want to reach out and touch her on the arm and say, "Is it really that perfect? Level with me. Sometimes, don't you feel you're carrying more of the load than he is? Sometimes, isn't it a little more than you can handle? Someday, you may wake up, as I did, and realize that all these years you've been doing what *he* wants you to do...not what *you* want." But I don't. She will never hear me because she isn't listening now.

"Your husband reminds me so much of Ronnie when he first started out in business. Don't let him teach you too much or you'll regret it," I warn with a touch of sarcasm. "You'll become indispensible."

Doris waves away my remark with a smile. I guess we all have to learn from experience. Take mine for example...

The year after high school, I commuted daily to Pratt Art Institute, an hour-and-a-half trip one way, from New Jersey to

Brooklyn. There were rarely any seats on the bus. I precariously balanced portfolio, pocketbook and 3-D projects through the morning rush hour. I never got a seat.

A couple of young men near the back of the bus caught my eye. They were regulars, too.

"There she is," said the guy with the dark hair loud enough for me to hear, "Wonder Woman." I pretended to ignore him.

"Nah," said the other one, "that's Mrs. Santa Claus." He was referring to my tasseled hat trimmed with white rabbit fur. I couldn't resist answering.

"If you guys were gentlemen, you'd get up and give me a seat," I teased back.

"Me? A gentle-man? I'm a working-man. I need my rest." The dark-haired one continued to poke fun.

"Yeah, sure." I juggled the hatbox containing my clay project. As the bus swayed, it narrowly missed his ear.

"Why don't you put that up in the baggage rack," he suggested not moving a muscle to help.

"Look, I can't reach." I stood on tiptoe to show him. "Besides, I'd never get it down again."

"You better go home and eat you Wheaties, Wonder Woman," he snickered. I was beginning to get annoyed when he added, "Well, the least I can do is hold it for you."

"Gee, I thought you'd never ask." My mother always said, *Be thankful for small favors*. I wasn't sure if I should trust this perfect stranger with the artwork I had worked on so painstakingly.

He looked like a gangster, a hood. He wore a dark brown leather jacket open down the front. His hair was slicked back in a duck-tail and he needed a shave. His brown gabardine pants were slightly pegged and he sported suede shoes with pointed toes.

As the bus reached the other side of the bridge, the mad scramble began. Everyone pushed and shoved his way off. I was glad to have extra help with my paraphernalia.

The A-train took us downtown. It was an express. By standing the portfolio against the wall of the conductor's cab it was fairly safe. The hatbox was another matter. My 'pick-up' stood between me, my artwork and the mob. I noticed he was very tall and thin, almost gaunt.

"We've got to stop meeting like this," I mumbled as he was pushed against me. "We haven't even been introduced." I could tell by his breath he was a smoker.

"Now you know what it feels like to be a sardine," he kidded.

Just then the train gave a jerk. "My project! It's getting squashed!" The sides of the cardboard box gave way like an accordion. "You...creep!"

"What do you want out of me? You ought to have better sense than to bring a monstrosity like that on the subway in the middle of rush hour."

"I can't help it if my class begins at nine o'clock. Do you know how long I worked on it? I was up 'till 2 a.m. sticking little toothpicks into those clay shapes. Or should I say lumps."

"They look real nice on my shirt. Thanks a lot! Here, have a stick of gum and drown your sorrows." He shoved a piece of Juicy-Fruit in my mouth. "By the way, I'm Ronnie. Who are you?"

"Judy. I'm sorry I called you a creep. But now I'll get an "*F*" for this project."

"My stop is coming up next," he said brushing off my apology.

"Where do you work?"

"American Litho. It's a print shop."

The express snaked it's way swiftly through the under-ground. 34TH STREET, the sign proclaimed.

"Okay kid, you're on your own."

"Thanks. Maybe next time we'll meet under less pressing cir-cumstances, ha, ha."

"Do me a favor and create in miniature next time."

"What, on the head of a pin?"

"Yeah!"

The pressurized door slammed shut and he disappeared into the crowd.

Not my type, I thought. His manners are atrocious.

Over the next couple of months we would run into each other quite frequently as we commuted into the big city. He always teased me in a flippant way. An attraction grew between us. I kept expecting him to ask me for a date. When he didn't, I began to drop hints.

"Did you see that new Walt Disney movie?" I asked nodding to the advertisement on the wall of the subway.

"You mean *Alice in Wonderland*? Sounds real exciting."

"You don't like Disney movies? I love them."

"Can't say that I do. What's it about? Some dizzy dame?"

"Don't you know the story of Alice in Wonderland?"

"Never heard of her." He examined the poster closely. "That's a nice print job. Must have been run on a four color press. Yeah. That's got class."

"So why don't you break down and take me," I said not letting him change the subject. I was getting bolder.

"To that silly-ass thing? I wouldn't waste my money." He was teasing me again, or was he? The verbal sparring continued over the next few weeks. It was spring when he finally broke down. "You really want to see that silly movie?"

"Yes, I do. Not just because of the story but to study the cartoon style, the art techniques. Did you ever see *Fantasia*?"

"No."

"The artwork was terrific. We all had to go see it for one of our design classes."

"So...okay, let's go."

"You mean it?"

"Yeah, I mean it. How about Saturday."

"You'll have to meet my sister, you know," I said.

"You mean I have to get the once-over, huh?"

"Well, I'm living with her and she wants to know who I go out with and everything."

"All right. I'll be over about 6 o'clock."

I didn't know how to explain Ronnie to my married sister. He didn't fit into any of the usual categories. On first impression she might think he just stepped out of a cops and robbers picture, a "B" movie. I felt I had to explain that this was just a date. After all, we had nothing in common.

Ronnie arrived late sporting his leather jacket. I was disappointed. I had expected he would dress up a little. At least he was clean shaven and his hair slicked back neatly in a D.A. (Duck's Ass, a popular style in the '50s.) He wasn't bad looking in a rugged sort of way.

He walked quickly toward the bus stop and I struggled to keep pace with him. This seemed like a strange date to me. He had no car.

"You know, you never told me your last name. I'm surprised my sister didn't pump you for it."

Ronnie smiled. "It's a little hard to pronounce. Can you say finger?"

"Of course I can say finger. Does it rhyme with finger?"

"Can you say jello?"

"It's Fingerjello?"

"Not quite. You have to get the 'gwa' sound in there."

"So tell me already."

"Frin-guel-lo." He rolled the "r" nicely. "The 'u' is like a 'w'."

"Fringuello. That's not so bad, except I can't roll my tongue. Harder than Anderson, my own name, but not bad. Is it Italian?"

"You bet your bippy."

"And I suppose you're Catholic?"

"Yeah, so?"

"My parents will have a fit when they hear I went out with a Catholic. We're Protestant."

"So don't tell them."

"I won't but my sister will."

"Where do your parents live?"

"Central Jersey. A town called New Egypt." It was my turn to be embarrassed.

"Sounds like a real hick town. Did you come to the big city to seek your fortune?"

I nodded. "To become a commercial artist. My mother wants me to be a teacher like her. But New York sounds more exciting."

"Are you good at drawing?" He pronounced "drawing" with a New York accent.

"You'll have to come up sometime and see my etchings," I said in a husky stage voice. He looked at me out of the corner of his eye to see if I was serious. I giggled. "Seriously, I wanted to be an artist since I was a little girl. I used to copy Porky Pig and Mickey Mouse. When I was a teenager my mother let me go to Philadelphia every Saturday morning to art classes at the Museum School. I had to commute quite a distance. Sometimes, I would take the bus on Friday night to my aunt's house in Moorestown and stay over."

"You traveled all alone?"

"Yes, for about five years."

"That's real dedication."

"The classes were excellent. I can remember some of the lessons in detail. I learned to stretch my imagination. We had one teacher who read stories about the Middle Ages and we had to illustrate them. I remember one poem.

From ghosties and ghoulies,
And long leggedie beasties,
And sounds that go bump in the night,
Dear Lord, deliver me.

I could see he was losing interest in art talk. I switched the subject from me to him. "And what about you? Do you like being a printer?"

"Yeah, I'm an apprentice on the two-color press and I'm learning to run the Multi. I must admit I'm pretty good."

"Okay, if you're so good you can print my Christmas cards next year," I teased. "Just show me how to prepare the art."

"Wait a minute. I said I was an apprentice."

"By next Christmas you should be a pro."

"Okay, you're on. But all kidding aside, someday I'm going to be so good I'll have my own business. There's a lot of money in printing if you have the talent and know-how."

"And I'm going to be a childrens' book illustrator. Hey, you can print the books I illustrate." We *did* have something in common.

Ronnie became involved explaining the techniques of the printing business. I could tell he was consumed by it. That attracted me. He was different from the others I had dated. He really cared about what he was doing. He had a goal. Not only did he want to be good at his work, he wanted to be the best. I admired his desire for perfection. He had big dreams and I could tell he wasn't afraid to work to attain them. The gap between us began to narrow.

The movie was fun but not one of Disney's best.

"Sort of crazy, don't you think?" Ronnie said.

"The colors were a knockout," I commented, not wanting to admit there was something lacking.

"A kid would be scared to death."

"Were you scared?" I teased.

"Sure. See, my hands are perspiring." He grabbed my hand and held it tightly.

We just made the last bus home. When we got to my stop I expected Ronnie to accompany me off. It was after midnight.

"Aren't you coming?" I asked getting up to pull the cord.

"This is not my stop."

"You mean you're going to let me walk home alone?" I asked in disbelief.

"How am I going to get home? This is the last bus."

"Take a taxi."

"Are you kidding? You think I'm rich or something?"

"Okay, then, so long." I wasn't going to beg.

Disappointed, I got off by myself and walked the rest of the way quickly. Not even a good night kiss, I fumed. I believed in being practical but this was ridiculous! He had deflated my ego.

The next few weeks I intentionally avoided meeting him on the bus. When he finally called I tried to sound cool and distant.

"I'm busy Saturday," I told him when he asked for a date. "I have another engagement."

"Okay," he said bluntly and hung up.

I was furious! He wouldn't even give me a chance to make him jealous. After a few weeks of moping I realized I was hooked.

It was his very unpretentiousness that did it. I began catching the same bus in hopes of meeting him again.

And that's how it started. A straightforward, unassuming relationship began.

I wanted to be a *real* artist that summer and go to Cape Cod to paint.

In my childhood fantasies I had pictured heaven as riding around the countryside on a horse and painting spectacular scenery. Not having a horse, I settled for a bicycle. I tried to talk my girlfriend into bicycling to Cape Cod with me. We could get waitressing jobs there for the season. I bought a second-hand bike and started taking short trips, but my friend chickened out. I decided it was too risky to go alone but I was determined to go to the Cape, anyway. The summer before I had been an elevator operator for a department store in Philadelphia. This year I wanted to get out of the city and back to nature. I sold the bike and bought round-trip train and bus tickets to Provincetown, Massachusettes. As soon as school was over in May, I set out with $65.00 in my pocketbook.

On the way up on the train I began to get a bad head cold. Maybe it was the excitement or maybe it was the air conditioning. By the time I'd ridden all day on the train and another couple hours on the bus, I was pretty miserable. The bus station in Provincetown was a diner. The suitcase I was carrying held all my worldly possessions. It weighed a ton. I had no idea where I would spend the night. I had a splitting headache and didn't know a soul. I persuaded the guy behind the counter to hold my suitcase for me while I walked around the town to get my bearings.

It was getting dark as I tramped anxiously through the windy streets, shivering under a spring jacket. Luckily, I found a place with a room for rent a few blocks away at the incredibly high price of $21 a week. I knew I couldn't stay there long because my money would never last. But it would do for a couple of days.

The next morning my cold was worse but in spite of it I was up early, canvassing the town for a job. What I hadn't bargained for was the Massachusettes "blue laws". I had to be 21 to work in an establishment that served liquor and I was only 19. I was very discouraged until someone suggested a restaurant on Main Street called *The Town Crier*. It was a glorified diner, open breakfast through dinner with an excellent menu of seafood. It was perfect and they hired me on the spot. At their suggestion I found a place to live not far away for only $7 a week. It was a tiny attic room, the bathroom was on the floor below but it had a skylight and a tiny balcony. I almost felt like a *real* artist.

I was an experienced waitress but I had a lot to learn. The girl who showed me the ropes was also in college. Amelia lived in Provincetown all her life and she had a New England twang. She was chubby, had straight limp hair, wore thick glasses and next to her I felt like Miss America.

"Do you see that customer over there?" Amelia whispered to me. "He comes in every morning. He can be real ornery. Has to have his eggs just so. Boiled two minutes, no more, no less. If they're not just right, he'll send them back."

"What about the chef? He doesn't seem the type to have things returned," I said nervously.

"Who, Rocco? Well, yes, he is a little high strung. But you do your job and you'll be okay."

Just then there was an outburst from the kitchen. Two waitresses came scurrying out with their pancake orders. One was almost in tears.

"He cursed at me for not picking up fast enough," she whined, trying to adjust her hairnet by looking in the shiny side of the silverware tray. "He's a crazy man."

My number lit up on the board over the door. "Must be my bacon and over-easy," I mumbled as I rushed into the kitchen.

"Where have-a-you been?" Rocco bellowed. "I been-a-calling you five-a minutes." His thick Sicilian accent hissed out between even white teeth and from under a bushy mustache. He was short and stocky with olive skin. His eyes were angry and flashed black sparks.

I grabbed my order and ran.

The next time I had to go into the kitchen Rocco was preparing the ingredients for the specialty of the house; baked, stuffed lobster. He had two huge butcher knives that he used to expertly dice the onions, garlic and celery on a wooden block. Wham! Wham! As he chopped he yelled out orders to his assistants who were breading the shrimp and scallops.

"Don't waste-a the egg, you ninny. Watch out for the shells. These shrimp are not clean." I watched in amazement as he took the pan of shrimp and dumped them in the sink. Suddenly, he whirled around and saw me.

"What-a you look at?" he screamed. "Don't just stand there."

"I...I need an order for French toast," I said finding my tongue.

"Oh m'god." he swore, "We ain't taking no more breakfast

orders. You hear?"

"But you have to. Mrs. Cabot didn't change the menus yet."

"I said NO BREAKFAST!" he shouted swearing in Italian, slamming the knives down faster and faster.

"Just a minute," I yelled back, "My customer specifically asked if we were still serving breakfast and Mrs. Cabot said 'Yes'. Now, damn it, I want an order of French toast."

CRASH! Rocco flung the knives into the chopping block so that they landed quivering straight up in the wood. He stood, hands on hips, glowering at me with those angry black eyes. I put my hands on my hips and glowered back with my Anglo-Saxon ones. I was trembling inside from the anger but I didn't flinch. After several long seconds of staring, he lifted his big white apron and carefully wiped his hands. Then, he leaned over the counter so that we were eye to eye.

"Okay but this is the *last* order," he said shaking his finger under my nose.

After that Rocco and I became best friends. He would shout and swear at me and I would shout and swear back. Whenever he fixed a special order, he'd save a little for me to taste.

"Try this. I make it for you," he'd coax. Some of the other girls began to get jealous of his attention to me. I got an education in seafood cuisine, Italian style. I also learned that fresh clams came in a gallon can from Japan already cleaned and the *just caught* Cape Cod lobsters were flown in daily from Maine.

Every day at 12 noon the boat from Boston sailed into the harbor and anchored at the end of the town pier. The town bustled with visitors who were trying to see and do everything in two short hours. Rocco and his crew threw pots and pans around furiously and we waitresses served platter after platter of piping hot seafood to eager tourists. They crowded the narrow, cobbled streets and jammed the quaint little shops that sold hand-made jewelry, pottery and leather crafts.

One shop owner was a handsome man named William, a deaf mute. He was a regular customer at our restaurant. His specialty was hand-worked leather sandals. He took impressions of your feet and molded the leather to it. We had a deal worked out where he sold them to us at a discount and we wore them while we worked. We were his walking advertisements. The craftsmanship of those sandals was of such high caliber they lasted for almost 15 years.

In my spare time I attempted some paintings in oils. One was an exaggerated view of the back door of the restaurant.

Everyone thought I was crazy to want to paint garbage cans. I was into the "ashcan school" of art. Another scene I painted from the balcony of my rooming house. It was difficult to get around because I didn't have a car. The beach was on the other side of the peninsula and the days I had off were either rainy or cold and windy.

By the beginning of August I was getting homesick. If I had hoped to meet an interesting companion I had come to the wrong place. There were not a lot of available males. I missed New Jersey and Ronnie. I tried to convince him to visit me and finally after much correspondence, he agreed to spend part of his vacation with me.

He arrived a day late.

"Why the hell did I let you drag me up to this god-forsaken place?" he growled. "Do you know how long it took me to get here?"

"You're going to love it here." I was delighted to see a familiar face. "I got you a room at the same place I'm staying..." Out of the corner of my eye I noticed someone listening to our conversation.

"Oh, yes," said Ronnie, "I want you to meet Charles. We met on the bus."

Charles was a pudgy, middle-aged man who wore bermuda shorts, support hose and sandals. He never took off his fishing cap the whole time he was there. He was on vacation and needed a room, too. So, Ronnie invited him to share his. Charles followed us everywhere. When we had our picture taken together, guess who was holding the camera? When we went to the beach, guess who carried the blanket? We never had the opportunity to be alone because Charles was always there. I think he had been sent in answer to my mother's prayers.

"Ronnie, can't you get rid of him tonight?" I begged through clenched teeth.

"But how? He doesn't seem to take the hint."

"I would like to be able to talk to you without him hanging around. He gets on my nerves."

"He's got nobody else to pal around with. Maybe they have a senior citizens' club around here where we can dump him."

"He's not *that* old. After work, let's go for a walk, *alone*."

About 10 p.m. Ronnie and I walked out on the town dock together.

"How did you manage to slip away from him?"

"I told him I was going to bed early." Ronnie put his arm around me and pulled me close. "Tomorrow's my last day."

"I know. I'll miss you."

"How soon will you be coming home?"

"I'm suppose to stay until Labor Day but I think I'll tell them I have to check on my room at Pratt and leave early. I really do, you know."

"You're going to live in Brooklyn?"

"Yeah. I have a deposit on a furnished room. It has a bed and a hot plate. That makes it furnished."

"Going from one attic to another?" Ronnie teased. I was getting use to his teasing. It was part of his personality. I began to see him as my *diamond in the rough.* I knew he must care for me a lot to have come all the way up here to visit me. I was sorry he was leaving.

We sat down on a bench at the end of the pier and looked out over the harbor. The moon's reflection stretched out in a rippling, sparkling path to the dark horizon. I snuggled up close to Ronnie and he put his arms around me. It was so romantic. Just like in the movies. Ronnie was kissing me on the neck when I glanced back over his shoulder toward the town. Under the streetlight stood a figure looking out to sea.

"I'm so glad you're leaving tomorrow, Ronnie," I whispered in his ear.

"You're what?" Ronnie pushed me away so he could look into my face.

"That means that creep is leaving, too, doesn't it?" I nodded toward the portly shadow. Good ole' Charles had perfect timing.

"Oh, my God," growled Ronnie. "Let's ignore him," He pulled me close and we continued our embrace. What happened to Charles after that I don't know.

The next day Ronnie and his traveling companion left for New York City. A few weeks later, I left, too. I said goodbye to Cape Cod promising myself I'd return next time as a tourist. The trip home seemed so much shorter. It had been a successful summer. I had saved some money, completed four paintings and learned that living alone was not as much fun as I'd expected.

The room I rented in Brooklyn was on the 3rd floor of a brownstone known at Pratt as "approved housing." It was filled with art students, all female, with the exception of a married couple who had just had a baby. The landlady lived in the basement and very seldom climbed the stairs because of her arthritis. When she wanted us, she would ring a bell that was attached to a long string that hung down the stairwell, four stories. Her disability was our convenience. Although all men were supposed to be out by 10 p.m., she seldom made the effort to check out all four floors. Needless to say, in this stimulating environment, art and romance blossomed.

In February, Ronnie and I decided to get engaged. The time had come to introduce him to my parents, a moment I had been dreading. I had to make up an excuse to bring him home to New Egypt for a week-end.

Daddy was a hard man to talk to. All during my teenage life he'd rarely carried on a conversation with me. It was no different now. Ronnie kept waiting for the right moment to break through the stony silence. Finally, as my father was driving us to a friend's house, Ronnie blurted out, "Mr. Anderson, Judy and I are getting engaged."

Daddy didn't say anything. He just stepped on the accelerator. We went flying down the road at 70 miles an hour. The next morning I could hear loud voices arguing in the kitchen. Daddy was expressing his views to Mother.

"If that's the way it is, then you handle it. I wash my hands of the whole mess." With that my father stamped out of the house slamming the door behind him. A typical action he used to express his frustration.

Ronnie slept blissfully on the living room sofa throughout the whole barrage.

"Did you hear that?" I asked nervously, shaking Ronnie awake.

"Wh...what?" Ronnie was still half asleep.

"Mom and Dad just had a fight. Didn't you hear him slam the door? I think he was a little upset over what we told him last night."

My mother tried to explain his actions.

"You know your father. Anytime there's a problem with you kids, he just walks out and leaves it to me."

"There is no problem, Mom. We just want to get married," I said with hesitation.

"Have you thought this through? Getting married is not all fun and games. You are both so young, only twenty. You're of different religions, different backgrounds." She was trying hard to make us understand.

"We can work it out."

"It's easy to say but not so easy to do, especially when you have children. How will you raise them? Catholic? You know the old saying, 'oil and vinegar don't mix.' "

"Oh, but they do," said Ronnie speaking up confidently for the first time. "They'll mix if you *beat* them hard enough." His remark caught my mother completely off guard. She offered very little resistance after that.

Ronnie's family was at the other extreme. His mother couldn't wait to marry him off. She was so eager, she was willing to pay for the wedding herself. She was ready to start making arrangements as soon as we announced our intentions. And of course, she expected us to move right in with her after the honeymoon. His parents had recently purchased a new house in the suburbs. They had come over from Italy over twenty years ago and worked long and hard saving every penny.

Typical immigrants, they started out on West 44th Street. Then, they moved to the Bronx while his father worked as a waiter in one of the finest hotels in Manhattan. In his spare time he served as bartender at the Metropolitan Opera. Pop was very distinguished looking with finely chiseled features. A crop of thick white hair and fair skin made him appear of Swiss descent rather than Italian. He was fastidious in his dress and wore his working tuxedo with dignity. He knew every opera by heart and on his day off would play his records and sing at the top of his voice much to the annoyance of everyone in the house, especially Mama.

Mama was a strong woman, determined and independent. She never spent time or money on herself. Her children, house and garden were more important, in that order. She kept house with a vengeance, making Marisa, Ronnie's younger sister, clean and wash ceaselessly.

In addition, she worked full-time in the textile industry. She made sure her only son went to the best private schools. If he wavered in his studies, she would engage a tutor. He took piano lessons three times a week. She insisted he had the touch of a concert pianist. It was a disappointment to her when he lost interest. Another disappointment was when he quit college after the first semester. Her goal for him was to become a doctor. But, by then, Ronnie had had it with books. He grew impatient and rebellious. When she realized she was losing her power over him, she decided he needed a wife to settle him down and keep him out of trouble. When I came into the picture, she was ready to shift some of the responsibility over to me...with strings attached.

The eagerness of one family balanced out the reluctance of the other. We did the most logical thing under the circumstances. We eloped! Both families were disappointed. By taking matters into our own hands, we were demonstrating our independence from them both.

It was a struggle from the beginning. But we were young and

healthy and took on the challenge with enthusiasm. Ronnie worked two jobs. We took in roomers and I cared for a couple of children of working mothers along with Leo, our first born.

When I became pregnant with our second child, Ronnie got the opportunity to buy a used printing press. We had to go into debt but it didn't seem to bother him. All he needed was determination, hard work and guts. Wasn't that the American way?

Ronnie continued his full-time job in the city during the day and ran the press on our enclosed front porch at night. I helped by making phone calls, ordering supplies, running errands, stripping up negatives, making line drawings and keeping the books.

When he offered to teach me to run the press, I declined. That was probably the smartest thing I ever did!

The business grew and so did our family. Tim was born. I forgot about my dream to become an illustrator. I was too busy to paint, too busy to even dream. My creative urge was submerged in procreation. I took my proper place beside my husband, helping him become successful. His success would be my success and we'd live happily ever after.

YOUTH'S DREAM

Ah, the dreams of youth!
They are like snowflakes in a storm
falling faintly at first and then.
caught in the whirling hurricane fly faster
and faster, until heaped in white drifts
upon the frozen ground
they slowly melt
away.

J. Fringuello

3

It's not my fault

"Have you all got your homework?" I called over my shoulder as I finished up the breakfast dishes. Silence at last.

Nothing rattled me more than this early morning rush. From the time the four of my children opened their eyes it was, "Lisa, give me back my blouse," or "Mommy, he's showing his food in his mouth at me," and "It's my turn to have the coupon on the cereal box!"

Finally, after a hectic hour of chasing down the mate to a brown sock, packing midmorning snacks, and inspecting outdoor clothing for missing parts, I opened the back door and the children burst forth like wild animals in a circus. I pictured myself as the trainer cracking the whip and the children as the lions falling all over each other as they crowded through the narrow exit of the ring.

I glanced at the clock. Just enough time for a cup of coffee and a few minutes to myself before I get ready for work. I go into the dining room and gently lift the still-wet oil painting off the piano and carry it into the kitchen. The light was better here in the doorway. I studied it critically as I drank my coffee. The only trouble is I've looked at it so much I don't really see it any more, I thought, squinting my eyes. I turned the painting upside down. There, that's better. Hummm. There was still something wrong with the background.

My ten precious minutes flashed by. I dashed upstairs. threw on some clothes and ran a comb through my hair.

Things were getting better at my husband's offset printing shop. It was such a struggle to be in business for yourself. The amount of hours spent never equaled out to the amount of money you could afford to pay yourself. And I hardly drew a salary at all. Just enough to cover a babysitter after school.

Business seemed to be picking up. I didn't have that constant gnawing, empty feeling in the pit of my stomach except when the accounts receivable got really high and the cash flow was out instead of in. Then, I would itch and start to break out in hives. I just couldn't take it when things got rough. Ronnie didn't really understand how I felt. He thought I was weak. Perhaps, he was right.

I was jarred back to 9:02 a.m. as the phone rang.

"Mrs. Fringuello?" says a nasal voice.

"Yes, this is she."

"This is Timothy's class mother. School will be closed today because the heating system is not working. It's 19 degrees this morning so we have no choice but to send the children home."

"Oh, all right. Thank you."

Oh hell, today my husband promised to make out bills. Now, they'll be late again. But it was a good excuse to stay home and work on my painting. It wouldn't be so bad after all. Here they come again, I thought, more like playful puppies this time instead of lions.

"Guess what, Mom? We get the whole day off 'cause the school's too cold," called Leo as he burst in the door. "When the principal told us, the big kids threw their hats into the air like this and shouted 'Yeaaaa'." He imitated their boisterous shouts, throwing his hat around the room.

"The teachers looked happy, too," interrupted Lisa.

Their happiness bubbled out in little giggles as they recounted the recent events. I marveled at their happiness. In a little while they would realize there was nothing exciting to do. It was too cold to play outside and when they became bored they'd start arguing and fighting. The only other escape was the TV and I'd be the big bad mommy for not letting them look at it twelve hours straight.

It's either me or them, I thought, as I switched on the morning cartoon show. "You can watch for an hour," I relented. They settled down on the floor in front of the set.

Gingerly I picked up the half-finished painting and retreated down to what I laughingly called "my studio". In one corner stood the washer, dryer and a perpetual heap of unsorted dirty clothes.

In a basket, an equally enormous but clean pile waited to be ironed. Over by the cellar door was a chest of drawers stored with summer clothes, boxes of hand-me-downs I was going to remake *when I got a chance* and a cabinet crammed with very used toys.

On the other side leaned an artist's easel next to a rickety table loaded with art supplies. Stacked along the wall were paintings and sketches, some framed. A florescent light cast an artificial aura upon the scene. The smell of oil paint permeated the cellar.

I squeezed out a new palette of colors. I mixed the white carefully into the green. The sick looking color reminded me of the hospital. God knows, I should remember the color of the walls. I had stared at them for four months or more. And I'd be staring at them in the future.

As I painted, my thoughts drifted back to that hospital room a few years earlier. Tim was five years old...

It was very quiet in the ward. All the children who were well enough had gone to the playroom on the top floor. The others, like Timmy, were too sick to get out of bed. The drawn shades tapped gently as a spring breeze filtered through the half-opened window into the darkened room. Tim tossed and fretted from the urinary tube they had found necessary to insert. I couldn't understand it. He had been able to pass urine before we brought him to the hospital. The only thing that appeared to be wrong was the blood in his urine. What had they done to him to make him hurt so? I cried silently to myself as I watched him. What had he done to deserve this? What had any of these children done?

In the next crib next to Timmy, a baby about 9 months old was strapped in a grotesque brace, his legs the shape of an arch. He had had an operation to correct a birth defect. He was born with his bladder outside his body. In order to put it back in place, they had to force his hips into the correct position by dislocating them. He lay on his back reaching for the mobile of gaily colored birds overhead. He could not sit up or turn without the aid of his mother or a nurse. His parents came everyday and were very attentive to him. When they left, there was hell to pay. The nurses would ignore his screams. Suddenly, they were too busy with someone else. Other visiting mothers would try to entertain him, even changing his soiled diaper.

At first, the smells and sounds repelled me but soon I found myself helping him and others who needed attention. This could be *my child* and I hoped someone would care for Timmy when I wasn't there as well.

Another crib was wheeled into the room. It contained a two-month-old baby just returning from the recovery room. Its arms and legs were tied down to the sides of the crib. There was a tube leading up through its nose and down to its stomach. Another led from its penis to a bottle under the bed. A third tube of blood plasma dripped into a large vein through the soft spot in the baby's skull. It was Timmy all over again. I turned away quickly, thinking, "And you thought you could be a nurse?"

Dr. Nilsson hadn't believed me when I'd called and told him I saw blood in Timmy's urine. He had just examined Tim for a preschool physical and pronounced him healthy. The only problem was that he still wet his bed. But that was not unusual for a five year old, claimed the pediatrician.

"Are you sure he didn't eat beets for dinner?" Nilsson quizzed me.

"No, I think it must be blood."

"Okay, bring him over to the local hospital and we'll have a look, take some tests."

It *was* blood. They began to run more elaborate tests. After two days I talked to Dr. Nilsson again.

"I really don't like the looks of this," he said, "I think you should take him over to a more comprehensive hospital, like the one in New York City. They can do a better testing job than here. Also, you can be admitted under clinic rates. If it turns out to be something serious it will be better for you financially."

I didn't realize at the time the importance of this statement. I was too stunned. Dr. Nilsson had made a wise choice.

Ronnie and I picked up Timmy the next morning. He was very upset and obviously in pain from the catheter they insisted he wear. Timmy squirmed and whined all the way to New York City. It upset me because three days ago he had been a normal, contented child. It wasn't until they treated him at the hospital that he began to act like this. What had they done to make him so uncomfortable?

Admittance to such a large hospital consumed the whole day. Finally, after being shuffled from office to office, we were allowed to go up to the tenth floor, the floor for childrens' urological disorders. What a relief after the interminable waiting to get away from the cold, indifferent attitude of the administrative staff. Once on the proper floor, the nurses were warm and friendly but, again, we had to wait for the doctor in charge of this department to see us. All the while Timmy cried and complained about the tube. I began to question its necessity.

I looked around at Timmy's new home. The ward was large and sunny. There were twelve cribs in little cubicles with glass windows. A TV at one end occupied several children in wheel chairs. Other children ran around in pajamas and slippers, some with plastic urine bags tied to their legs. I was surprised the nurses didn't seem to mind them being out of bed. One baby in a crib sat with his feet sticking through the crib bars, crying softly.

Finally, all was in order and we had to leave. I said goodbye to Timmy reluctantly. I knew we had to leave him here for his own good. But it was such a big, impersonal place for a five-year-old. We reassured him that Mommy would return, tomorrow.

The following day when I checked in at the desk, a nurse told me that the doctor wanted to see me immediately. My stomach did a flip-flop. The doctor was a tall, imposing woman. She took me aside into a supply room where we could talk privately.

"You must explain to your son that we are not playing games here," she said. "We are trying to help him." Her steel gray eyes penetrated mine. "He won't let us touch him. He keeps screaming, 'My mother doesn't want you to do this!'"

I listened, secretly applauding Timmy. I felt my anger rising at her insensitivity. "It's the catheter. He says it hurts him."

"Impossible. It's a child's Foley catheter. There's a little ballon inside that is inflated after it is inserted. Once it's in place, it doesn't hurt a bit."

I wondered how many catheters she had endured. "But he doesn't usually complain about things. I'm sure there must be something wrong. It must be irritating him. Is it really necessary?"

"We don't do unnecessary procedures. He is not in pain. He is just upset about being here. Please explain to him we must do this." Her sterness convinced me.

"Yes, of course." My heart ached and I wanted to take his place. Oh God, give me the pain.

I found Timmy's bed and gave him a hug. He was still fretful and unhappy. "It hurts, Mommy, it hurts. I want to go home."

I gritted my teeth. "Timmy, listen to me. We brought you here so that they could make you well. Dr. Nilsson says this is the best hospital. They have to keep in the catheter. The doctor is the boss here. Not Mommy. Not Daddy. What the doctor says, goes. Do you understand?"

He acted like he hardly heard me. "I want to go home."

After a few days they finally realized that the balloon that held Timmy's catheter in place was irritating his bladder and giving him real pain. They changed it and he was comfortable at last. Now maybe they would listen when he complained.

For many days I waited for someone to talk to me about Tim's condition. The nurses, especially the young ones, tried to be kind. But no one could answer my questions, no one could give me consolation. All I knew was that he was having tests. Tests, for what?

On Friday, the head nurse told me that Dr. Armstrong wanted to talk to me. I was to hear something at last.

We sat at the octagonal playtable on hard little chairs in the center of the ward. The doctor shuffled a pile of papers, the results of Timmy's tests. He was a gentle-looking man, more like a scientist than a doctor in his immaculate white coat and horn-rimmed glasses. He had a kind face, one that I wanted to trust so badly. I was surprised to see the eyes of the head nurse look at me in a softer-than-usual manner. It alarmed me. Was it sympathy?

Then, I heard. The words tore at my ears, ripped at my heart.

"It's really a shame this wasn't detected earlier. We might have been able to correct it. You see, for some reason, we don't know why, the urine has backed up the ureter tubes and damaged the kidneys. There's only a tiny part of each kidney left that's functioning. Right now, there is a tremendous pressure on them. He can't go on like this much longer. We have to take emergency steps to relieve the pressure immediately or it will be too late."

I put my head down and sobbed. The words swirled around and around. It can't be too late! I just had him for a physical. Dr. Nilsson had said he was doing so well. There must be a mistake! The tests are wrong! I was very faithful about getting him shots and check-ups. When he continued to bed-wet I had him checked out, more than once and by different doctors. Everything was negative. Why hadn't anyone detected this in time? Was it my fault? It couldn't have been my fault. I had done everything a mother should do and more. Why hadn't the doctors found it out in time? *It's wasn't my fault!*

The nurse and doctor tried to sooth me but I felt like I was smothering. I *must* give permission for the operation, they said. A tube would be implanted through his lower back directly into his kidney. This would relieve the pressure temporarily. The tube would drain into a bottle or a portable plastic bag strapped to his leg.

They shoved the permission slip at me. Sign here. This hereby gives the hospital permission to do whatever they deem necessary to save his life. With a stroke of the pen, I committed Timmy into their hands. How easy they made it sound. "Don't blame yourself," they kept repeating, "it's just the way things happen. It's nobody's fault." A searing flame of resentment and guilt began to burn deeper and deeper inside me.

Timmy had fooled them all. They didn't expect him to last through the first operation but he did. Then, they inserted a tube into his other kidney because there was still so much pressure. The first time I stayed in the hospital waiting room off the main lobby. They forgot I was there. The second time I stayed at home. They could notify me just as quickly by phone. That way I could look after the baby and keep busy so I wouldn't have to think about it. Poor Donna. She was beginning to wonder who her mommy really was. Every day someone different took care of her.

Ronnie took me into the hospital that night after the second operation. Tim was still groggy with anesthesia. I stroked his head gently and called, "Tim-Tim." With a great struggle he tried to open his eyelids but they were so heavy. A faint smile flickered and faded.

"C'mon," said Ronnie. "We can't do anything for him. He doesn't even know we're here."

He was right. There was nothing I could do. Ronnie was uncomfortable in this place, anxious to leave. The saline solution dripped slowly. A nurse was timing the drops and regulating the delicate control. "Take care of him," I whispered hoarsely as Ronnie led me firmly away.

The next day, I went to the lobby window and showed my pass. "Oh yes," said the girl at the desk finding Tim's name on the list. "Timothy has been moved from this ward to a private room downstairs. We had to put him in isolation. He has the chicken pox."

Chicken pox on top of an operation? I wanted to laugh and cry at the same time. How ironic! I donned the white mask and gown and stepped into a tiny white room with one window, a cell. The view was a brick wall. It didn't really matter. Tim was so miserable he didn't want to eat, to talk, to play the radio, to be read to...nothing. He just wanted to be left alone. He really frightened me. I thought, God, this is it. He's going to die. But about a week later, he started to perk up and complain about the food. I was relieved. He was coming back to the land of the living.

Tests, tests and more tests. Two months went by. Tim had

so many x-rays we joked about him becoming radioactive. Every day, the lab technician came around and pricked a different finger and drew some blood. Most of the other children would put up a fuss. But not Timmy. He wrapped himself up into a tight little cocoon. I would talk to him and he would act like he didn't hear me. He was withdrawing into a safe little world of his own where there was no pain.

One day, right after lunch, we were seated around the play table with several other children. The lab technician arrived with his little tray of test tubes, cotton balls and alcohol. He proceeded, methodically, to call off each child's name and to work his way around the table. As his finger was stuck, each child would put up some resistance, fuss a little and then go back to playing. Then, the technician would move on to the next victim. He was getting closer and closer to Tim.

"Timothy Fringuello."

Suddenly, Timmy froze. His face began to turn purple and he began to scream hysterically. That was it! He had had it! No one could calm him down.

I begged the doctors to let him come home. "Please, can't you see he's cracking up? Those dark circles under his eyes haunt me. He needs to sleep in his own bed again, have a home-cooked meal. If he stays here any longer, we'll both go insane." At last they consented.

It was not until the instructions began that I realized the awesome responsibility I would have. I wanted him home. We all did. I would be able do something for him at last, but the task before me was overwhelming.

Tim's tubes had to be irrigated daily. I had to force sterile saline water up into the tubes with a syringe, also sterile, to clean out any pieces of mucus or other debris that might block the tube. At night, each tube was hooked up to sterile bottles on each side of the bed. Every few days the gauze and tape which held the tubes securely in place had to be changed. There was a yellow discharge which oozed out of the opening around the tube. This had to be cleaned and new bandages applied, a technique in which I soon achieved a high degree of dexterity. I was proud to have my son declare I did it better than the nurses. He would call for me when we went to the clinic.

Every care had to be taken not to pull on the tubes. A sudden jerk and they could come out. Then, we would have to drop everything and rush him back to the hospital. The tubes must be replaced immediately under sterile conditions. If too much time elapsed, the opening would close up.

Every month we reported back to the clinic to change the tubes. Sometimes, he would run a fever the next day. He was on medication constantly to cut down the risk of infection.

In spite of all the precautions, I was determined to return Tim to a normal routine. It was a summer of mixed feelings. On the one hand I was weighed down by the constant care he needed but on the other hand it was a joyful release. How wonderful to leave the prison cell. Tim and I were liberated, at least temporarily. Our family could *live*, not simply exist.

Timmy blossomed. He ate and played and slept...awoke to play and eat some more. The circles under his eyes disappeared. Listlessness was replaced by bouncing boy-energy.

Although he was not allowed to go swimming, he could run joyfully in and out of the waves playing "can't catch me". His new found energy was spent digging in the sand, searching for sand crabs, collecting buckets of shells, enjoying the wind and sun as only a six year old can. I held my breath each time he climbed a tree or wrestled with his brother but I knew I couldn't act too protective or he would grow into an emotional cripple. Well-meaning friends and relatives questioned me when they saw some of his antics. They thought I should wrap him in cotton and keep him in a safe little shell. But, I couldn't do it to him. I had to let him have his freedom. Ronnie felt the same way. We would take our chances.

A PARADOX

I ask God
To keep him well
And he is sick.

I ask God
To spare him pain
And he suffers.

I ask God
To save his life
And he dies.

I ask God
To take my life
And I live.

In despair
I beat my breast
And cry aloud to God.

Afraid,
Unanswered,
My faith grows deep.

J. Fringuello

4

A bill of rights

That September, we enrolled Timmy in kindergarten complete with urine tubes and plastic leg pouches. His teacher was kind and understanding without being overly solicitous. He walked the six blocks every morning to school with his brother. His trousers covered the plastic pouches and no one guessed he had problems.

The future hung over us like a specter. I tried not to think about it because it was too frightening. In November, we had to report back to the clinic for another evaluation.

At the hospital, the line moved slowly up to the cashier's window. I tried to juggle my clinic card, money, pocketbook and overnight bag and at the same time hold Timmy's hand. The cashier stamped the card, handed me change.

One the third floor I looked around at the huge waiting room. Rows and rows of cold metal chairs stood empty. I knew they would soon be filled. The line began to grow behind me. Mothers with children of all ages...babies, toddlers, school age children, all waiting.

Finally, at 9 o'clock, the line started to move. Why does the woman at the desk have to be so nasty? She looked like a dried up prune of a woman with sharp features. She acted like she was doing the world a favor by caring for the poor and sick. God forbid someone should ask a question or have a receipt out of order. She must get her kicks by talking down to people. And if she detected an accent, you didn't stand a chance.

Time passed slowly. Timmy amused himself with coloring books and pretzel snacks. The clinic slowly emptied out. It was past twelve o'clock. Timmy began running up and down the aisle for drinks of water. I didn't have the heart to make him sit down. We were among the first people to arrive and now we were almost the last.

Finally, we were called. I began to fill out the admittance forms while the intern examined Tim. Included in the paperwork was the standard permission form that permitted the hospital to perform operations and procedures that they deemed necessary. I filled out everything except the permission slip.

The aide checked through the papers and handed it back to me.

"You forgot to sign this."

I pushed it firmly back. "I didn't forget. I'm not going to sign it now."

"Oh, but you have to sign it or the hospital won't admit him," she said pushing it back to me.

"But, I'm not going to sign this until I've talked to the doctor in charge of Tim's case."

The aide became flustered and more aggressive. "Mrs. Fringuello, this is for your own good. Just suppose there is an emergency in the middle of the night. You wouldn't want to be called down here just to sign a form would you? Think of the inconvenience." The speech sounded rehearsed.

"I'm sorry. That's the chance I'll have to take. If I do sign it I won't be able to sleep *any* night. I want to talk to the doctor first to find out exactly what they are going to do to my child."

The aide still didn't understand the point I was trying to make. Stunned, she got up and called the head nurse. Now it was two against one. They had the advantage and they knew it.

"Don't you care about your child?" The head nurse disdainfully applied pressure.

I had been very calm up to this point but something inside me snapped. "Of course, I care. Do you think I would be here waiting for hours if I didn't care? Look," my voice rising in deliberate anger, "the last time my son was in the hospital, I watched a mother go into shock as she saw her month-old child come back from the operating room. No one had told her the surgery was to be performed that day. No one had bothered to pick up the phone and call her. I'm not going to let that happen to Tim or me."

My protests fell on deaf ears. "We can't possibly admit Timothy unless we have your signature." An icy barrier froze between us.

"Then, I want to talk to the doctor in charge. I think he will be very upset if Timothy doesn't show up today."

The nurse, visibly perturbed about this snag in the machinery, flounced into the inner office to call upstairs. A few minutes later she was back. Furiously, she gathered up all the papers. Turning to the aide she said, "Take Mrs. Fringuello up to Pediatrics. Dr. Lynch will accept *full* responsibility."

I grabbed Timmy by the hand and quickly collected our belongings. End of round one, I thought sheepishly.

It was almost like a home-coming. The nurses greeted Timmy warmly. There were a few new faces and a lot of old familiar ones. And there was Anthony. He was about the same age as Timmy, curly haired, dimpled, an adorable imp. His parents lived quite a distance away and didn't visit him often. But that didn't seem to bother him. He made friends with everyone who walked into the ward. He also wore a tube but unlike Timmy his future was hopeful. Together, the two of them kept the nurses hopping.

They would watch monster movies on TV together, play games and when they were feeling good, drag race the wheel chairs down the long hallway. The nurses seldom complained of their antics.

One day I came in to find them both restricted to their beds. "Why does Timmy have to stay in bed today?" I questioned the floor nurse thinking he must have a fever.

The nurse gave me a haughty look. "Tim and Anthony are being punished."

"Oh, too much running around?" I really wasn't surprised. I would have lost patience long before this.

"No, not that," she said, a hint of a smile playing across her face. "We had complaints from the first floor guards. The boys took the rubber examining gloves and made water balloons out of them. They threw them out of the 10th floor window!"

I turned around and frowned at the boys. They were busy trying to see who could hang no-hands from the pole that held the privacy curtain in front of their beds. A couple of unconcerned monkeys.

After the usual week of testing, Dr. Lynch, the urologist, requested a conference with Ronnie and me. He was an intelligent man, personable yet professional, respectably keeping his distance. He didn't talk down to us but laid out the problem in layman's terms making it easy for us to understand. We sank back into the plastic cushions of the dark green lounge chairs on the sun porch and listened.

"Timothy's case has been carefully evaluated. With nine doctors on the staff, of course, there is some difference of opinion. We all agree that we can't keep on like this because the chance of infection is so great. One of the advantages of a big teaching hospital like this is that no one doctor ever makes a decision alone."

And the disadvantage, I thought to myself, is the constant change of personnel, especially resident doctors.

"Several of the older doctors," he continued carrying the conversation efficiently, "feel that nothing should be done, that he doesn't have that long to live. A few believe that his bladder is probably unusable so a by-pass should be made. You see, there is and has been, in all probability, a partial blockage at the mouth of the bladder from birth. The urine backed up the ureters, the tubes leading from the bladder, and damaged the kidneys. The bladder worked overtime to try to empty itself. In some places it became very thick and muscular, in other places very thin almost to the point of perforation."

"What is involved in a by-pass?" asked Ronnie.

"That would mean severing the two ureters and bringing them together at an opening we would make at his waist. He would have to wear an apparatus, a plastic pouch that would catch the draining urine. He would never use his bladder again. However, *I* want to try something different. I believe that through a series of operations his bladder can be repaired. I would remove the obstruction and eventually, through surgery, return him to normal. Of course, we can't be sure we will be successful. We don't know the extent of damage to his bladder."

"And what about his kidneys?" Ronnie questioned zeroing in on the real problem.

"Unfortunately, the damage to the kidneys is permanent. However, a person can function on a very small portion of the kidney. Tim will be able to get along very well with what he has until he's about thirteen."

"Thirteen? And then what?" I listened anxiously.

"Well, it depends on how fast his body matures." Lynch started to hedge. "We don't really know but several members of the staff feel he does not have enough functioning kidney left to become an adult. His lifespan is limited."

A series of operations and he still won't make it past thirteen? I felt cheated for him. He would spend half of his life in the hospital and still die.

"If you do it now, what about Christmas? Will he make it

home in time?"

"Oh, yes," Dr. Lynch's tone became most confident. "I'm sure he'll be home for Christmas. We will only do the first operation."

Ronnie and I exchanged glances. Promises, promises. We were both thinking the same thing. I took another look at Lynch. He was really enthusiastic about this operation, maybe too enthusiastic. Did he realize it was my child's life he was experimenting with so willingly? Was it my imagination or was he pushing just a little too hard in favor of his idea?

"Do we have to give you an answer right now?" Ronnie was stalling so we could talk.

Lynch shuffled his papers. "We'd like to schedule him for early next week. Why don't you take the week-end to think it over and call me Monday. In the meantime, we'll tentatively schedule him for Wednesday morning."

I hesitated. "You won't do anything until we sign a permission form, will you?" The urgency I heard in his voice made me uneasy.

"Oh, no, of course not," the doctor's said in a patronizing manner. "Don't worry. He won't go into surgery until both you and your husband agree to this."

That was the problem. Ronnie and I couldn't agree. Ronnie felt the doctor's decision was a good one.

"They want him to be normal," he argued.

"So do I. But you know and I know he may not make it home for Christmas. You know the kind of delays and complications that come up in a situation like this. Not to mention the red tape. Ronnie, I don't think I can take much more of this. How can I do all the Christmas shopping and keep running to the hospital every day? You know how hectic it was last time. The other kids need our attention, too. Leo needs help with his reading. I would have to get sitters for Donna and Lisa."

"But what other choice do we have?"

"Why can't they wait till after Christmas? There's really no emergency. He's waited this long, what's another month? In this way, if something drastic happens..."

"Nothing's going to happen."

"But you heard Lynch. Some doctors prefer to do nothing. They think he's going to *die*. It could happen during surgery. I don't know how the kids and I could make it through Christmas if that happened."

Ronnie was getting impatient. "You're always so dramatic."

"Life and death *are* dramatic."

"Then *you* make the decision. Be your usual obstinate self."

He left the house in a huff. He had an important job on the press with a deadline. As owner of his own business he had to produce or we wouldn't eat. *Obstinate self.* His words stung. It was easier for him to submerge himself in his work and let me thrash out the problems. I resented his ability to escape. The walls were closing in on me.

I sat down at the piano. I had once been able to play a little but had never found the time to keep it up. I noticed an old hymnal in the pile of sheet music. I leafed through it and found an old favorite I remembered singing as a kid in the Baptist Church. *What A Friend We Have In Jesus.* All alone and feeling sorry for myself, tears began to stream down my face as I read the words...*All our sins and griefs to bear/What a privilege to carry/Everything to God in prayer.* I needed a friend. Someone who really understood how I felt. This burden of responsibility was too great for me to bear alone. God, I prayed, help me make the right decision. Let this be your decision, too. Don't let me be selfish or obstinate. I want to do what's best for Tim and for all of us.

As my emotions intensified I imagined the eye of God looking down at me, a giant orb that seemed to engulf me and burn through my tears and into the very center of my brain. Suddenly, a great calm came over me and I was at peace. I knew that it would be all right to postpone the operation. Inspired, I picked up a pencil and paper and wrote the following letter to Dr. Lynch:

> *Dear Dr. Lynch,*
>
> *If I for one moment could believe that this operation would save his life, I would insist upon you doing it immediately. But Timmy has been living on the brink of disaster for some time now.*
>
> *My responsibility being to the whole family, I cannot in good conscience permit it now. Do you realize what havoc just his being in the hospital plays with our family life? Suppose something should happen during the operation. I would never forgive myself for not giving Timmy "this Christmas" at least. And what kind of a holiday would it be for the rest?*

That was the last we ever heard from Dr. Lynch.

Timmy came home and preparation for Christmas took on new meaning. The children's excitement heightened as the day drew near.

When Christmas Day arrived the toy that made the biggest hit was a green monster on wheels powered by a battery and controlled by buttons from a long cord. With careful coordination you could make him roll forward, lean over and pick something up. It was good for grabbing someone unexpectedly by the leg.

Timmy had a great time sending it after the dog, knocking down his brother's log fort and scaring Donna out of her wits. I guess it was his way of getting even.

One night, a few days after Christmas, Tim rolled over in bed and pulled out one of his tubes. I quickly arranged for a babysitter and prepared for a run to the hospital. We spent over an hour in the clinic wading through administrative procedures. They couldn't find his chart. Then, when they realized he needed a specialist, we had to wait an hour more.

Finally, a resident doctor appeared, another strange face. I explained the situation as briefly as possible. As he flipped through Tim's chart, a growing accumulation of test reports and doctors' summaries, I felt as if I knew more about what was needed than he did. The nurse sent for a sterile setup.

The doctor's hands shook as he opened the package and picked up the tube with the forceps. I tried to comfort Timmy. He knew it was going to hurt and he tensed up. The doctor fumbled and dropped the tube on the table. I could hardly believe what was happening as he picked it up and proceeded to insert it as if nothing had happened. After all I had been lectured about the necessity of sterility? I watched dumfounded as he continued to foul up the job. It was evident he had never done this before. Even I knew he should be using a smaller tube. Every misguided probe made me wince in sympathy for Timmy. Finally, I could contain myself no longer.

"How can you do this to him?" I shouted. "The tube is no longer sterile. You call yourself a doctor? If you don't know how to do it, then get someone who does!" I flung myself out of the room so inflamed I couldn't see clearly. I couldn't stand his ineptness and Timmy's cries. His pain had become my pain.

"Where's Dr. Lynch?" I asked the nurse outside.

"You have to understand that it is the holidays and this resident is the only doctor on call. Dr. Lynch won't be with us as of January 1st anyway."

Another kick in the head. Lynch was leaving? Of course!

I should have known. The residents change every six months. So *that* was why he was pushing the operation. Things began to make sense. It was as if a light bulb went on in my head. This little experiment on my son would have been a feather in his cap before he moved on. Maybe my prayers had been answered more fully than I expected.

When the doctor finished I went in and wiped the tears from Timmy's face. The waste basket was full of bloody cotton swabs. In these days of medical miracles why does there have to be any pain?

When Timmy entered the hospital in January, I was prepared to do battle. I wanted to know everything they were going to do and why, in detail. I was not going to be manipulated this time.

I was disarmed when I met Dr. Gardner, the Dr. Kildare of Pediatrics.

"We believe Timmy's bladder can't be salvaged. I am going to do just one operation. It will be the last one he will ever have to have."

The magic words, *Tim's last operation,* spread over me like anesthesia, numbing my mind.

"It will be a by-pass, as was explained to you before. The ureter tubes which normally lead from the kidneys to the bladder will be sewn one into the other and an opening made for them at his waist." His voice made things sound soothingly simple.

"What will happen to the incisions they made for the plastic tubes?" I asked.

"They will slowly close and heal. There will be much less chance for infection. He will wear an appliance to catch the urine. You will have to help him adhere it and see that it is cleaned properly. During the day it will be concealed under his clothes and no one will know it's there.

"At night he will hook the bag to a tube and drainage bottle. His output of urine is twice that of a normal child because the kidneys are not getting the wastes out efficiently as they should. We will keep him on a medication called Gantracin. You'll have to bring him back monthly to the urology clinic for checkups."

"Is the outlook for the future the same as before?" I was looking for a miracle.

"I'm afraid so," said Dr. Gardner weighing his words cautiously like a miser weighing his gold, fearful of giving away a fraction of hope. "As his body grows, what is left of the kidneys will not be able to handle the waste it produces."

"I've been reading about the possibilities of kidney transplantation. Do you think..." I was not giving up. I was grasping at even the wildest idea.

"Tremendous research is being done in that field. Unfortunately, it is all experimental. I doubt if we will see it take place in our lifetime." Dr. Gardner was adamant.

Although we were disappointed that Timmy would never again be physically perfect, we were glad this would be the last time he would have to go through such painful trauma. I was sure my prayers had been answered. He was not going to be subjected to any lengthy, untested procedure. With adjustments, he would be home to stay. Things could get back to normal.

But in spite of feeling we were doing the right thing, on the day of the operation I felt depressed and saddened. When I thought of him and his poor little mistreated body, I pictured him already dead. Perhaps, deep down, it was what I really wished for him, an escape from suffering. The same questions kept repeating themselves. Why had Tim been chosen and my other children spared? Why? Why? As I waited to hear from the hospital, I felt very near to God.

"Well, God," I said casually, as if He were sitting in the same room, "I guess you'll be calling for Timmy soon. Could you save him a grassy hill, maybe? With wild flowers and crawling bugs and things, where he can run and shout? A little stream at the bottom would be nice, where he can catch tiny black minnies or collect smooth white stones that will spark when he strikes them together. Perhaps you've a stretch of sunny shore with an ocean for him to splash in. He loves to dig and make sand castles and look for shells.

"And on rainy days, that is if you have them up there, a piece of string and a couple of rubber bands will keep him busy. Or if you have any stray cats...

"Take him. He's yours. He always has been. We sure appreciate you letting us have him these six years. Take good care of him and please, God, don't let him hurt again. He's had more than his share down here on earth.

"I know You'll get a big kick out of him when he comes running and yells, 'Hi-ya, Dad!' We'll miss that special sparkle in his eyes. Please Lord, forgive me if I cry."

But God wasn't ready for Timmy yet.

COME and WORSHIP

Oh, come and worship at the Shrine of Medical Science,
Remove your shoes and bow your head with humble mien,
    You tread on hallowed ground;
What miracles are performed in the name of medicine,
The blind can see, the lame pick up their beds and walk.

Oh, come and worship at the Shrine of Medical Science,
Behold the priests in white who stride with dignity,
    Far above the deplorable masses;
Pay tribute to their skill so sure, precise,
A small price to pay for the rewards so great.

Oh, come and worship at the Shrine of Medical Science,
Come, bring your children for holy sacrifice,
    Lay their innocence upon the altar;
With their blood, the wicked are purged,
The evil spirits are cast out.

Oh, come and worship the world's advance in Medical Science,
How far removed from the barbaric rituals of the Incas,
    The ancient wizardry of Greece;
Look back with scorn for this is the True Salvation,
Oh, come and worship, come and worship.

                                        J. Fringuello

5

Cinquain

The view from the bedroom window was magnificent. The early morning sun touched the snow-capped Alps and they shone like the Golden Apples of the Hesperides. The air, frosty yet laden with the promise of spring, lifted my spirits and renewed my strength. The last four years had been difficult. At last there was time to think, time to sort out past events and put them in an orderly sequence.

Mama had sensed I desperately needed a change. At her invitation I packed three month old Amy, diapers, formula and all, and flew with her and Ronnie's parents to Italy, back to the little village of their birth, leaving Ronnie to manage the other four children.

I thought about Timmy constantly but I knew Ronnie could handle any emergency. I took my problems, bundled them neatly and placed them in the back of my mind for temporary storage. It was time to heal myself.

The village of Masserano was as old as civilization itself. It was built on top of a high hill, as were most towns in northern Italy. In ancient times this natural barrier protected them from the enemy who could be spotted miles away. Besides, it was unhealthy to live in the lowlands. The dampness and mists were evil and diseased. Near the center of the town was the church. The steeple reached high into the sky like a sentry. Here, the church, along with the religion it represented, was decaying.

There were pieces missing in the designs of the stained glass windows. The vacant places let in light and rain and birds. During the poorly attended services there was much flapping, cooing and chirping overhead.

Beneath the religious fortress was said to be secret tunnels winding down and out into the valley, escape routes in time of danger. When the Germans came, resisters slipped away undetected.

In some parts of the village, the buildings dated back before the time of Christ. They leaned heavily upon each other, their great age hidden in layers of white-wash like the powder on wizened prostitutes. Sometimes, you could see faint traces of frescoes, a Madonna's face, a faded Christ child, reminders of their past virtues, shimmering through the mold-covered plaster. It was not the art of Michelangelo or a Raphael but primitive art with a Byzantium flavor. The quality didn't seem to matter to the villagers. It was art and they worshiped it. On a ledge in front of a painting they would place a candle or a jar of fresh flowers making it into a shrine, not because they were pious but because they loved art and what it stood for. They were all aware of their great history, of their contribution to the world's culture. Even the most ignorant, the least educated understood and were proud of their heritage and ashamed of the deterioration that lay around them.

When our plane landed in Milan, I didn't notice any difference in our surroundings. We sped north along the four lane super highway. It could have been an early spring day anywhere. The land was very flat. Fields of rice stretched out as far as the eye could see. I felt like we were passing through the potato farmlands of Central Jersey.

Then, I began to become aware of the contrasts. The roofs of the houses were made of deep orange tile. The walls were not painted one monotonous color but two and three, some pastel shades, some bright. There was humor in the choice of the parts painted, each house seeming to outwit the other in originality of placement. There were motorcycles, motorbikes, three-wheeled carts everywhere. As we crossed a narrow bridge I looked down at a group of women washing clothes in a stream, their sheets spread out on the rocks. They wore long black skirts and scarfs and they waved and gestured animatedly.

We were jammed in the little car. Uncle Leo had borrowed a neighbor's Fiat and the neighbor came along as driver, partly because he didn't trust anyone to drive it and partly because he didn't want to miss anything. Including cousin Renata, there were six adults and the baby plus the luggage.

Suddenly, the highway ended and a secondary road began to climb sharply. As one, we swayed together as the car whipped around sudden turns and winding curves. Piedmonte was an appropriate name for the province, *the foot of the mountain*. I caught an occasional glimpse of the Alps hazy in the distance.

Leonardo, Mama's brother, had a brand new house. His wife Lena willingly gave up the biggest bedroom to us and proceeded to make us welcome. Where she and Leonardo slept during our three week visit I was never sure. Half of the house was still unfinished inside and unheated. I have my doubts whether she slept at all. She waited on us hand and foot, cooking two big meals daily.

The baby and I adjusted nicely to our surroundings. I had to insist that I would care for Amy myself or Lena would have taken complete charge of everything. Little did I realize that this was the treatment I needed. Involuntarily my memory would flash back over the past nine months...

It had been the lowest point of my life. A year ago I had been so hopeful. All four children were in school. Timmy acted like any normal, well-adjusted child of ten. He had come through the ileostomy operation with flying colors. Although the urine bag was a nuisance he seemed to accept it as a matter-of-fact.

The printing business was holding its own. I had lost some weight, was exercising daily and felt fit and confident. I decided it was time to go back to school to complete the degree I had started at Pratt.

Then, I found out the news. I was pregnant again!

It started out with excruciating pain and blood. The doctor at the emergency room thought I was having a miscarriage. But he was wrong and I was furious at his misdiagnosis. I called my own obstetrician for advice.

"I don't understand how I could be pregnant. It's impossible," I said angrily. "We took every precaution. And I'm worried about the bleeding."

"A lot of women have spotting the first few months. It's nothing unusual."

"But isn't miscarriage nature's way of getting rid of the abnormal, the malformed?"

"Yes...that can be true but..."

"Well, maybe my body is trying to get rid of an imperfect child. You know what I have been going through with Tim. They said his problem probably started with a congenital birth defect. Suppose there is something wrong with this one, too? I couldn't go through it again with another one. I just couldn't." My voice went higher and higher as panic set in. "And the future is so uncertain with Tim. No one knows what may happen."

Couldn't he see what I was driving at? Didn't he understand what I really wanted was an abortion? Did I have to spell it out for him? I couldn't, try as I may, bring myself to say it. The word "abortion" stuck in my throat. I kept throwing the ball to him but he wouldn't catch. He tried to calm me down.

"Now look, get a hold of yourself. There's no reason to believe this baby won't be healthy. What Tim has isn't hereditary. You got off to a shaky start, that's all. Lie down and let someone else do the household chores for you. I'll send over something to relax you."

Yeah, sure, a tranquilizer. Take your pill, put your feet up and call me in nine months. Not very likely. There was no one in the family available to help me with the house and kids and I couldn't afford to pay someone. The kids do help out a lot but I couldn't make them responsible for everything. Somebody had to shop, clean house, cook and wash. Did he think I could afford a maid?

Why did I have to pick such a conservative doctor? I was just starting to get a little control over my life and this happened. There must be somebody up there pulling the wrong strings. I couldn't believe this was happening to me. If I wrote it all down it would sound like a friggin' soap opera. Maybe, I should shop around for the right kind of doctor, an abortionist. But I wouldn't know where to start. My minister? Forget it. All I'd get is a sermon. My mother? Nice girls don't talk about such things. I couldn't take another "I told you not to marry an Italian" look.

Even if I did find a doctor, I probably wouldn't have had the guts to go through with it. Something deep down inside me knew it was not right. I guess I'm not a risk taker, a gambler.

I was so angry with those doctors who just stood by twiddling their thumbs doing nothing. They could see my mental state of mind was not stable and yet the only thing they offered was something to calm my nerves. What did I have to do, slash my wrists to show them I was serious? With the amount of tranquilizers I'd need, I'd be a drug addict by the time I was forty.

The injustice of the situation rolled round and round inside me like a steel ball in a pinball machine bouncing off one hurt after another, accompanied by the flashing lights of guilt and the ringing bells of resentment. I knew no matter how much I shook the machine, no matter how skillfully I tried to wham those flippers, I'd never get a free game.

Ronnie didn't say much. He knew there was no point arguing with me. He was as surprised as I was at the news. He jokingly called it our "immaculate conception," especially since the baby was due on Christmas Eve. But I was in no joking mood. He listened patiently as I cried and complained night after night.

"Look at this house. Where in the world are we going to put another child? We can barely squeeze in the six of us. At least *now* it works out right, two boys and two girls. They share bedrooms and clothes. But look at the gap between Donna and this one, six years! It's embarrassing. And what about the dinner table?" I said encompassing everything with a sweep of my arm.

"Yeah? What about it?" growled Ronnie.

"Well, look for yourself. We all fit comfortably around it now. Six is just right. What will we do with seven? It's an uneven number."

Ronnie threw his napkin down in disgust. "For pete's sake, will you shut up?" he snapped. "We'll find room for it. I found a place to keep it for nine months, didn't I?"

It was as if he had poured a bucket of cold water over me. I burst out half-laughing, half-crying. I should have been insulted by his remark. It wasn't *his* body that would be twisted out of shape for the fifth time. *He* wouldn't be the one to endure the labor or get up at 2 a.m. after it was born. I should have been angry but I wasn't. There was a limit to the amount of sympathy he would give. He knew I had wallowed in self-pity long enough. I knew it, too. To continue would be to lose my sanity. Ronnie was my touchstone. Whenever I needed a dose of reality, I could count on him to fix me up.

Okay, so I go through with it. I'll have this baby. But damnit-to-hell this will be the last baby, I swore. I'd make sure of that. I'd find a doctor who would tie my tubes once and for all. They could take their tranquilizers and shove them. And God, I thought, are you listening? *This kid better be healthy!*

The next six months were the worst ever. The spotting stopped and I began to blow up like a balloon. The doctor threatened not to tie my tubes if I gained too much weight. I knew he was only trying to scare me. I tried to stop eating but his remarks reinforced my feelings about male chauvinist doctors.

I needed new maternity clothes because I had given all mine away in an optimistic moment. Rather than buy, I borrowed and scrounged. As the baby grew large within me, I became more depressed and lethargic. It was an effort to do the simplest household chore. I cried at the least little thing.

The children had never seen their mother cry before. At first I tried to hide the tears. Then, as the last month approached and I became more uncomfortable, I cried openly. Sharp pains stabbed at my back and abdomen, the veins in my legs bulged. I kept working at the shop a few hours a week to keep my mind busy and off myself in spite of my lack of energy. I knew Ronnie needed me to handle the bills and payroll.

There was only one way out of this mess. I wanted it to be over and done with as quickly as possible. The last time, with Donna, I had natural childbirth. I didn't go to classes or anything. I just practiced mind over matter, a sort of homespun hypnosis. It would never work this time. Because I was having my tubes tied I would have a spinal. What I really wanted was to be put under with anesthesia like sodium pentothal, way, way under.

The baby didn't wait for Christmas Eve. I started to get labor pains a week early. Please, not false labor like I had with Donna, I prayed. It was Friday night and I rushed to make out the payroll, to get to the bank and to order pizza for the kids' supper before letting Ronnie drive me to the hospital. He had barely returned home to his pizza when the phone rang. It was a girl. It was Amy. And she was healthy! And in a simple procedure I was free forever.

As if to make up for the trouble she had caused, Amy was the happiest, cuddliest baby of the five. She smiled from the moment she came home. Her chubby pink face peeped through the receiving blanket like a cupie doll. She loved to be loved. Maybe it was the guilt of not wanting her in the first place, maybe it was because I knew she was my last child but I loved her back...honestly. What had been a chore with the others was suddenly a pleasure. She learned to sleep thought the night immediately. She ate well and was contented.

The girls were excited about having a new baby sister. Lisa couldn't wait to get her hands on her. She considered herself surrogate mother. Donna felt unsure of her place in the family. She had been the baby quite a long time. On Christmas morning as they lined up according to age to go downstairs to see what Santa had brought, she asked plaintively, "Can I still go first?" The boys accepted Amy with a "so what's one more girl" attitude and Ronnie was as proud as if it was his first.

Once in Italy, Amy was the center of attention. Everyone made a big fuss over her. There hadn't been any babies in the family for a long time. Lena teased me by asking if I was going to leave her there when I returned home. In the old days this had been the custom. Those who went to America to work would send their children home to Italy to be raised by the grandparents. When the children were old enough to hold a job, they would rejoin their parents in the United States. It made me realize just how much Amy meant to me.

Lena was teasing but deep down she meant it. She had retired from her job in the textile mill a few years before. In Italy, retirement age was 55. She'd dedicated herself to cooking, cleaning, gardening and caring for her new home. She had the energy of two women and welcomed the diversion of the baby. Proud of her new house she pointed out to me that the kitchen was modern like in America.

In my eyes it seemed peculiarly small, or *pechinine* as they say in Italian. The refrigerator, the sink, the gleaming white cabinets were all scaled down as if made for Snow White's dwarfs. The stove was an interesting combination of two lifestyles. On the one side was bottled gas, on the other, a wood burner. The constant heat from the wood stove warmed the kitchen and on the back of the stove sat a pan of fresh milk pasteurizing slowly. Next to it was the indispensable soup pot. Every drop of water used in cooking was added to the pot. Leftovers were not refrigerated but dropped in and left to simmer. The sauces and gravies made from this reservoir were a gourmet's delight.

Pop and Uncle Leonardo began their day with coffee that smelled so strongly of liquor my stomach turned from just sitting next to them at the table. Pop was in his glory. He had dreamed of this visit for 20 years. Everywhere he went he would recall old times with his buddies and have a drink. He would discuss the state of current affairs and have a drink. He would ponder the future with his wife's relatives and have a drink. He never drank alone. All during the visit he was very happy and very drunk.

Mama clicked her tongue at him but did not nag or lecture him like at home. She was too busy. The first week she translated every word of conversation for me. The relatives asked a million questions. They oohed and aahed over a picture of Mama's house, Ronnie, Marisa, the grandchildren. The second week Mama only translated those words directed at me that required my answer. Sometimes, she would fill in her own answers without consulting me. By the third week, I was on my own. I picked up a few words and snatches of phrases but for the most part I guessed by the facial expressions and the tone of voice. I nodded and smiled a lot.

Living at the old homestead was Mama's mother. She was over eighty. The old woman was cared for by her youngest son, Joseph and his wife, Andreina. They had a daughter about eight years old. We were invited to dinner there on Sunday. One room served as living room, dining room and kitchen. In the center of the table, cooling on a wooden slab, was a huge mound of what looked like yellow mashed potatoes. It was polenta, the Italian version of our corn meal mush or grits. It was sliced and served with chicken cacciatore. No part of the chicken was wasted. Even the head and feet were in the serving dish.

The old one did not eat much. She had no teeth. She was content with a bowl of milk and bread. Sitting at the head of the table, the family showed their respect by serving her first. I sat next to her. All through the dinner she kept up a steady chatter. I would smile and nod my head politely.

"Nona, why do you keep talking to her?" Mama asked her in Italian. "She doesn't understand anything you are saying."

"Oh, yes," said the old lady sharply. "She understands, she understands." She turned to me and spoke as before patting my arm with her withered hand.

Before the visit was over, I felt completely at home. The faces around the table could have been my own aunts and uncles from New Jersey. They were all hard-working people, only of different ancestry. In spite of a language barrier, there seemed to be no difference between us. We were held together by a common bond of humanity.

One day I took my watercolors and went on a painting foray. There were so many picturesque spots it was hard to choose. What looked like a deserted building turned out to be inhabited and I felt strange working with curious faces surrounding me. I finally settled for a lonely place on the outskirts of town. Later, when I showed them the finished painting they snickered because the barn I had chosen to paint turned out to belong to Joseph. Inside was an outhouse. We all had a good laugh over my choice of subject.

Within this sheltered environment, devoid of pressures, tension and anxiety, the jagged edges of my old self began to heal. After two and a half weeks, I began to look forward to going home. I started to make plans and think constructively about the future. I was ready to step back into the time-frame of the world to which I truly belonged and face the problems that loomed ahead. Amid promises to return soon with Amy, we left Masserano and Italy.

When we got to Milan for the flight home, we learned the plane would be delayed because of thunderstorms over Rome. Graciously, the airlines treated us to a full meal with all the trimmings. The waiter offered to store the baby's bottle in the refrigerator until it was time to leave. Papa, over Mama's objections, polished off a full bottle of Chianti.

The 747 airliner landed about 200 yards out in the center of the field. Because it was so late they were eager to take off immediately. Everyone scrambled to gather up their belongings and raced out to meet it jumping over puddles left by the recent rain. Mama grabbed the baby leaving me to steer Pop's now well-petrified body out to the plane. Pop didn't want to go. Every time I grasped his elbow, he jerked it away. With much coaxing and prodding I dragged him out to the jumbo jet.

No sooner were we aboard than the door began to close and the engines rev. Horrified, I suddenly remembered the baby's formula still in the restaurant's refrigerator. I called out loudly, "I forgot the baby's milk," but the Italian stewardesses didn't seem to understand my English. The plane began to taxi. The only two Italian word I had learned well popped into my head and I screamed, "Bambino! Latte! Bambino! Latte!!" The planes engines slowed, the door opened and in a few minutes a little baggage car scooted out with the baby's formula. Little Amy had interrupted the schedule of a major airline.

LAST CHILD

One more
And that makes five;
As my reflection glares
I brush the broken straw
From off my back.

J. Fringuello

6

A real artist at last

I was happy to be back with Ronnie and my family. The nicest thing about any trip is coming home. It was good not to need a translator but it wasn't long before the old problems returned, with a vengeance. This time I could look at them with new insight and optimism. I had found the strength to face what lay ahead.

Ronnie continued to struggle with the business. It was like riding a roller coaster. That winter Pop became chronically ill with cirrhosis of the liver. When he died in February, the business was at its lowest ebb. Customers owed us thousands of dollars in back bills and we didn't seem to be able to collect them. Ronnie continued to work feverishly, bearing up under the shock of his father's death, hoping things would right themselves.

I'd never understood the purpose of funerals until Pop's. The ones I had attended seemed so emotionless and cold. Everyone was very solemn and spoke in whispers. I learned that an Italian funeral is not meant for the dead but for the living. It is alive and warm, a very human drama. At center stage is the widow, dressed in black and clutching several large white handkerchiefs, preferably men's. Around her arc the immediate family some propping her up when she feels faint. The deceased lies in an ornate casket covered with flowers. As relatives and friends arrive, the same scene is enacted over and over. First the widow kisses and embraces them. Then, she tells of his last moments alive and, as if on cue, the tears flow, the knees buckle and there is more clutching and hugging all around.

While this is going on up front, the rest of the audience gathers at the back and enjoys a grand old reunion. Stories are swapped, births announced, marriages recalled and good times relived. Between her performances, the widow joins in the festivities. On the day of the burial, everyone goes back to the house for a huge buffet surpassed only by a wedding banquet.

For three days Mama was the star. She played her part beautifully. No one could hold a candle to her.

After the first day, the funeral director pulled Ronnie aside nervously. "The suit you brought for your father?" he said pausing to clear his throat.

"Yeah, it looks good on him. You did a good job on the makeup, too," said Ronnie not giving him time to finish.

"What I mean is, did you notice the casket is only open half way?"

"Oh yeah, I was wondering about that," said Ronnie.

"Well, are you aware you only brought the jacket?"

Ronnie gasped, "You mean Pop is lying there in front of all these people without his pants on?"

"Yes, I'm afraid that's true."

"No wonder he has that little smile on his face!" Ronnie could hardly keep from laughing out loud. In his hurry, he had dropped the pants to Pop's good suit in the back of the van. Poor Pop, who was always impeccably dressed, who wore a tuxedo to his job as bartender at the Met, was buried without his pants.

A tall gentleman, well-dressed and dignified, came up to Ronnie and stretched out his hand.

"You don't remember me but I used to stay in your parent's back bedroom on 44th Street when you were a little tyke."

Ronnie clasped his hand. "Really? There was always someone sleeping in there, some cousin or another but I never knew who they were."

"Your father helped me enter the U.S. back in 1935. He got me a job as waiter with him and vouched for me. If it hadn't been for him I might not be here right now," he said, slapping Ronnie on the shoulder. "I couldn't count how many others he helped."

Ronnie looked at me. A new respect swept over his face. "I never realized. Pop must have been their godfather."

Another man introduced himself as Pop's partner, Julius. "We worked together 25 years at the hotel," he said sadly. "He was like a brother to me. I know more about you than you do yourself. That's all he talked about, his family. How many kids you got now?"

"Five," said Ronnie.

"Oh m'god, that's what I thought. And your sister, she got five, too?"

Ronnie nodded.

"You know your father didn't believe in life insurance." His tone became confidential. As he talked he reached into his breast pocket and pulled out a billfold. "He told me everything. Before he took the trip to Italy, he gave me this and said I should give it to you or your mother if anything happened to him." The man handed Ronnie a scrap of paper. On it was scrawled a symbol. "He said to be sure to look here."

"What does it mean?" Ronnie asked, dumfounded.

"I think it means he has some money hidden somewhere in the house. Your mother doesn't know about it. Did he ever hint around to you about it?"

"No, never. This is the first I've heard about it."

"Well, he seemed to think this would take care of everything."

When the funeral was over and everyone had left, I nudged Ronnie. "Don't you think you should give it to her? It's rightfully hers."

Ronnie pulled out the carefully folded paper. "Mom, did Pop have any insurance?"

"Not a blessed penny," she began. "All he has is the death benefit from his union. It will hardly cover the casket." She was on the verge of another scene.

"Did Pop ever tell you he was putting any cash away anywhere in the house?"

"No, why?" She sat up straight with a jerk, her eyes as dry as the Sahara Desert.

"Well, at the funeral, Julius gave me this. He said Pop told him you should look here." He handed her the paper with the hieroglyphics.

She contemplated it for a moment. "That son-of-a-gun. He held out on me? M'god, he told me he give me every penny."

"What do you think this means?"

"Maybe he just went a little crazy."

"You don't think he put anything away for a rainy day?"

"No, impossible. He was always good. He always give me everything, everything." She took the paper and brushed our questions aside.

Later that night, Mama took a flashlight and searched every corner of the house. She even pulled out insulation in the ceiling of the cellar. Under the eaves in the attic, laid neatly in packages, she found $5,000 in cash. It wasn't until she had spent over half of it on funeral expenses that Ronnie found out. As he looked through the remaining bills, he noticed they were silver certificates, all in perfect numerical order. Over the years, Pop, as a waiter, had carefully saved them from his tips without Mama's knowledge.

"You mean you've spent them already?" Ronnie asked annoyed with her secrecy.

"I had to pay the bills, didn't I? You think it's going to come down from heaven, out of the sky, maybe?"

"But Mom. these are worth more than face value. Each dollar is like a buck-fifty."

"Oh, m'god. Your father did this to me. He's dead but he's still causing me trouble."

"No Ma. *You* blew it"

To make matters worse, when cleaning the stereo where Pop used to play his opera records, Mama found another cryptic note. She figured he must have hidden more. Again, she scoured the house and ripped things apart. But, this time she found nothing.

"That's Pop's revenge," said Ronnie gleefully. "He knows she'll never sell this place if she thinks there's money hidden somewhere." And Ronnie was right.

The seriousness of our financial situation hit me one day as I borrowed the last quarter from the kid's piggy bank to buy a loaf of bread. What was I doing? Were we so bad off that I had to take the childrens' spending money to put food on the table?

The business was going nowhere. I really couldn't blame Ronnie. He was trying. He was putting in twelve to fifteen hours a day. Sometimes he would work all night. He was never home. If success depended upon hard work, we should have been millionaires years ago. He believed in what he was doing. I'd never dream of asking him to do anything else. The business was his life. I loved him for his drive, his single-mindedness of purpose, his commitment. To ask him to change would be like asking him to admit defeat. It would kill him. He would never be a 9 to 5 man. He was an individualist, a creative thinker in his own way. Perhaps, too creative and too honest for his own good, at least for the printing business. I felt like the business was a sea of piranha trying to eat us up alive.

No, I couldn't ask him to change. *I* had to be the one to do something and I had to do it quickly. If only I could bring in some extra cash for a few weeks to get us out of this bind, so that we could at least eat. We had borrowed up to the limit from the bank. It would be too embarrassing to ask my parents for help. They had helped us enough already. If we asked Ronnie's mother, she would insist we move in with her. I had been fighting off that prospect since we first were married. I would surely suffocate under those circumstances. I could just imagine five kids trampling her flower beds.

No. The only solution was for me to get a job. But what and where? There were only two things I felt qualified to do well; cut a straight hedge and pin a tight diaper. As I searched the classified section of the newspaper, none of the job titles seemed to be within my capabilities. *Dear God,* I prayed, *show me the way.* What would I do with the baby if I found a job? Amy was fourteen months old now. I'd have to arrange for a full-time babysitter. That part I'll work out later, I figured. First, I should concentrate on getting a job.

The only job I felt I could handle was as a nurse's aide. The next day I applied at the nursing home, a half-hour drive away. They seemed eager to hire me. The shift would be 4 to midnight, I'd earn about $75 a week and I'd have to buy a uniform and shoes. Maybe Ronnie's sister, Marisa, might have an old uniform I could borrow. She once worked in a doctor's office. I stopped at her house on the way home and explained my predicament. As always, Marisa cut to the heart of the problem.

"Why do you want to work as a nurse's aide?" she asked, her clear blue eyes opened wide. "You must be able to find something more suited to your abilities than that."

"I've looked through all the papers. There's nothing else I qualify for," I answered, my exasperation beginning to show. I had made up my mind and didn't want to be diverted from my chosen course. "Besides, it will be only temporary."

"Wait a minute. I thought I saw something under 'artist' just today." She picked up the newspaper and began to scrutinize the classifieds. "Here it is."

"I saw that one, too. But I have no experience," I protested.

"What do you mean, no experience? What about all the years working for Ronnie? They should count for something."

"But how do I explain what I do to anyone? I don't type well or take shorthand. I'm not really a bookkeeper. I just sort of muddle through. I can do a little bit of everything but nothing that could be given a job title, unless it's Girl Friday."

"You know a lot about printing, don't you? You're very talented at drawing and painting."

Yes, but..."

"So why don't you try for this job?" She shoved the newspaper under my nose. *Artist, wanted to do filmstrips.*

"I don't even know what a filmstrip is!"

"You'll never know until you give it a try." Marisa said with her usual innocent optimism.

I couldn't argue with her. She was right. What did I have to lose? I called the number listed and made an appointment.

Seated in the lobby under the receptionist's nose, I felt awkward and unsure. I wondered why I had let Marisa talk me into it. I wasn't really an artist, a commercial artist. My portfolio held sample of recently printed jobs as well as ancient renderings from art school. I didn't know which would be the more appropriate.

The interview went well. I was amazed that Mrs. Schaefer was impressed with my work. I began to feel a little more confident. She showed me examples of filmstrip art. They were small, full color illustrations of historical stories suitable for use in elementary schools. The art technique didn't look very difficult. In fact, I knew I could do better. And it looked like it would be fun to try.

"What does the position pay?" I asked trying to sound nonchalant.

"Oh, in the vicinity of $150 a week," Mrs. Schaefer said without batting an eye.

My heart jumped. It was twice what I would earn as a nurse's aide and not nearly as demanding physically. It was too good to be true.

"If you give me a chance I'd be willing to start at $125," I said. I wanted the job badly. "If you are satisfied with my work, you can raise it to $150 within a few months. And let me try my hand at a few frames at home to see if I can do it."

Mrs. Schaefer agreed. She was delighted that I was willing to start for less.

I had solved the most difficult problem, the job. Now I had to find someone reliable to care for the baby. My good fortune continued. My neighbor and long time friend, Marie, was willing to accept the responsibility. I knew Amy would be well cared for. My faith in the power of prayer grew.

Ronnie was surprised but skeptical. He didn't object to me working. He just didn't think I could handle it. "Even if it's only for a month," I said excitedly, "we're bound to come out ahead." He admitted I had a good argument but I knew he thought I was lacking in ability. The old male chauvinist attitude was showing. I had to prove him wrong.

On my first day of work, Amy was running a temperature of 102 degrees. Laden with guilt, I brought her over to Marie with the pediatrician's phone number and a list of instructions. I was determined nothing would stop me this time.

The company that employed me was a book distributor that published lists of books, visual aids and conducted book fairs for local schools. I was the first full-time artist to be hired to produce illustrations for educational filmstrips. My first assignment was, *Lief, the Lucky.* I had to research the Viking period of history, make pencil sketches and then do 8 x 10 renderings in color, always following the supplied script carefully. There were between 40 and 50 pictures, or frames, per script. I was pleased with the work and Mrs. Schaefer seemed to be pleased with me.

Getting ready for work was not so pleasing. I had to be at work by 9 a.m. Fortunately, it was only ten minutes away so I was able to get the four off to school before I left. I made them responsible for preparing their own lunches. Each was assigned a chore. Marie fed the baby after I dropped her off. One of the biggest time savers was disposable diapers. Pampers should be classified along with the wheel as man's, no, *woman's* most valuable invention. Next on the list is perma-press.

Ironing was out of the question, now. As soon as the clothes came out of the dryer, one of the kids popped them on hangers. There was never a build-up of wrinkled clothes waiting to be ironed, a depressing sight. From then on, I never bought anything that couldn't go in the dryer. I began buying one-size-fits-all socks for Ronnie and the boys, all the same color, black. I tried to accomplish the entire week's shopping on Saturday morning except for bread and milk. There were times when good humor ran out and tempers flared.

Coming home from work was the most difficult time. In the evening, amid the confusion of four chattering voices all seeking attention, Amy would take out her tiredness by screaming and hanging on to my leg as I tried to prepare supper.

It was hard, it took a lot of juggling and a lot of cooperation, but it was worth it. It made the children independent. It made *me* independent. I looked forward to going to work. It was creative and *an escape*. I was doing something worthwhile. Ronnie had to adjust more than anyone. The children were used to me working at the shop. If they had a problem after school they would call me up. Now, their father had to handle it.

"Can I go over to Jimmy's to play?"..."Timmy won't let me look at TV."..."I fell off my bike and I think my toe is broke,"...sob, sob. Ronnie had taken me for granted. I had handled the payroll, made out checks, bills and estimates. Now, I didn't have time or energy to keep it up. His part-time secretary took over most of my work and he began to write out checks himself. We had several confrontations before it penetrated that I had quit the printing business for good.

A year later Ronnie was able to boast he had done more business after I left than anytime before. I was glad for him and even more glad for me. If it hadn't been for the financial bind we were in, I never would have had the courage to make a clean break from the business.

At my job I worked enthusiastically and soon there were three other artists under me. I was given the title of Art Director along with the promised raise. My experience in the printing field came in handy as we designed promotionals, flyers and catalogs. Besides filmstrips, the company began to publish "easy reader" books. Illustrations were executed in two colors. I had the opportunity to write and illustrate several of these books. How exciting it was to see my name in print. *Written and Illustrated by Judith Fringuello.* My childhood dream of becoming a *real artist* had come true.

Live all you can; it's a mistake not to. It doesn't so much matter what you do in particular, so long as you have had your life. If you haven't had that what have you had?

Henry James
from
The Ambassadors (1903)

7

Wanderlust

Tim was twelve years old. The last few years we had tried to avoid doctors as much as possible. His condition had stabilized and I felt the less he was poked and prodded the better off he was. Maybe his kidneys had miraculously healed themselves, I prayed silently to myself.

But one day, he had a spurt of blood from the stoma, the opening in his side from which the urine drained. He was upset and concerned. Reluctantly, like a startled ostrich, I pulled my head out of the sand and made an appointment at the clinic. A new doctor, Dr. Wiley, was in charge now.

"Timothy's kidneys have failed to visualize on the x-ray. We need to do another I.V.P. (intravenous pyelography). I want to admit him to the hospital, immediately," Dr. Wiley insisted.

I could see Tim's face cloud with disappointment at the mention of hospital. Summer vacation had just begun. I quickly evaluated the situation. How many years had he been living like this? It was a twist of fate he was here today.

"Now wait a minute," I argued, taking a stand for my son. "I know all about his kidneys. I've known about them since he was five years old. Didn't you read his chart? We've been planning to go on a camping trip to Virginia, our first real vacation in years. Tim and the whole family are looking forward to it. We would never leave him behind. As soon as we get back, I'll bring him in and you can do all the tests you want."

"You're taking a terrible risk," said the doctor, his voice rising in urgency. He wasn't used to having his decisions questioned or his orders disobeyed. "Don't you understand? On the x-rays where his kidneys are supposed to be, there's nothing!" Several nurses gathered around shaking their heads. We were making a scene.

I took a deep breath. "It'll only be for a week. I'm sure for that short time he'll be fine. We could always find a hospital if there is an emergency," I said firmly. I wasn't going to let his scare tactics frighten me.

Dr. Wiley threw up his hands dramatically. "Mrs. Fringuello, you are taking your son's life into your own hands. It's up to you. The responsibility is on your shoulders."

I could feel the blood rush to my head. Responsibility! He should talk about responsibility! He should have walked in my shoes the past seven years. How dare he insinuate I didn't care about my son!

But in spite of my indignation, his words punched through my defenses and began to pummel that old guilt complex. I looked at Tim. His eyes pleaded with me. I pushed aside the doubts, curbed my anger and said evenly, "Let's go, Tim. I'm starved."

With great pleasure, Tim and I left Dr. Wiley standing there in disbelief, holding his x-rays.

"Did I do the right thing?" I asked Ronnie as we sat having coffee and cake after dinner. The kids had cleared the table and we had a few minutes to ourselves. I reached out for his reassurance.

Ronnie reflected as he took a bite of danish. "Does Timmy act any different than usual?"

"No, except he is excited about the trip."

"Has he lost his appetite?"

"Are you kidding'."

"Does he have a fever?"

"No. I can usually tell if he's getting sick by the dark circles under his eyes. But Dr. Wiley says..."

"Wiley says. Wiley says do this, do that. To hell with Wiley. It's Timmy we're concerned with. Do you think Wiley knows Tim as well as we do?"

"No, this is the first time they met."

"Well, then, let's go camping." Ronnie made it sound so logical.

Ronnie and I had decided to plan a camping trip for the whole family to the Blue Ridge Mountains in Virginia and we were going in style! Our red Dodge van hauled a rented Apache trailer. It opened up into a tent with two double beds, a tiny ice-box, a propane stove and a sink. Luxury, indeed! After checking and rechecking our supply lists, we were off. We hoped to make Maryland by nightfall. The Garden State Parkway lay like the yellow brick road before us. It would have been perfect except for a little black cloud of worry that hung over me.

"Hey, we're on our way," Ronnie bellowed in disbelief. He thumped the dashboard in time to the radio.

"How many hours do you think it will take to reach our first stop?" I asked pouring over the map.

"Who cares about time? We're on vacation. When we get there, we get there."

I could see Ronnie was starting to unwind. We were under-way at last. The kids were settled. I looked back at them fondly. It was nice to see them contented and not quarreling. I wondered how long it would last. Probably through one and a half comic books and a bag of candy.

Leo, the oldest, was getting tall and gangly. He was built like his father, thin with muscular shoulders and arms. His dark complexion made him look more Italian than his brother. His inquisitive nature made him hard to live with but I excused this as artistic temperament.

Tim hadn't really started to grow yet. He had freckles and fairer skin like my side of the family. Other than that he didn't look like me. His nose was small and pointed. I always wondered, with a bit of envy, where he got his nose. He was well coordinated and held the promise of an athlete. His mischievousness, coupled with Leo's inventiveness, made them quite a pair.

Lisa's straight black hair and olive skin were definitely not mine. The boys thought she acted like me, though, bossy and nagging. I could count on her to tell me if they were acting up. I trusted her completely with the baby even though she was only eleven. She had her father's ability to make friends and was well-liked at school.

Donna looked exactly like Ronnie's baby pictures, especially the one of his first holy communion. The three older ones picked on her and she cried easily. Although in some ways she seemed to lack common sense, she showed them all up by getting excellent grades in school.

Amy was the only one who resembled me in the least and that was only when she smiled. She was two and a half now and we left her with Grandma Anderson so I could have a real vacation. I settled back in the seat and tried to relax.

We had gone about fifteen miles, traveling about fifty mph, when all of a sudden Lisa yelled, "Hey, there's a wheel bouncing across the highway," and at the same instant there was a loud bang, crunch and s-c-r-a-p-e!

"What's happening?" I screamed to Ronnie as he gripped the steering wheel and fought for control.

"I think we got a flat!"

The van screeched to a stop on the shoulder of the road near an underpass. Everyone was shaken but unharmed. Ronnie got out to look for the problem. He came back scratching his head.

"The whole wheel is missing on the trailer. We were riding on the axle. We're lucky. It doesn't seem to be damaged and no one was hurt."

"Daddy," Lisa butted in. "I told you I saw a wheel go bouncing across the highway. It jumped off the roof of one car and another car nearly ran into it."

"That must be our tire."

"Ronnie, you're not going to cross the Parkway, are you?"

"How else can I get the wheel? Everybody sit tight. I'll be back in a minute."

My heart stopped as I watched him sprint across three lanes of oncoming traffic. I held my breath as he dodged cars in the northbound lane. Oh, God, don't let anything happen to him.

Ten nerve-racking minutes later, he was back with the wheel.

"The lugs snapped. We'll have to wait for a tow to a service station. Then, we'll call the place that rented this bomb to us."

It wasn't long before a tow truck came to our rescue but it seemed to take hours to get to the repair center, a noisy, busy garage. By then it was noon. No place to spread out the picnic lunch I had prepared so carefully. The kids were starved so, ignoring our surroundings, we dug into the basket of goodies. This was not exactly the idyllic scene I had pictured, eating salami sandwiches in a broiling hot truck.

The mechanics in the station hustled about. No one seemed concerned about our predicament. Ronnie called the rental people but they didn't know what to do either. We waited. Everyone continued to avoid us. All I could think about was the ice as it melted in the cooler.

"This is ridiculous," Ronnie fumed as he paced. "They don't have any wheel lugs this size or any suggestion as to what to do. We'll be here all day and tomorrow, too. There must be some place I can get bolts." Ronnie unhooked the trailer from the van and drove off looking for a hardware store that might sell bolts the right size.

It wasn't long before he was back with a suitable substitute. He borrowed the power tools and had the wheel back on the trailer snugly in place in less than ten minutes. We paid the outrageous towing fee and were back on the road again. This time it didn't look so magically yellow. The morning exuberance had turned to late afternoon impatience.

"We'll never make it to Maryland tonight," I griped.

"So look on the map for a campsite that's closer. How about Delaware?"

I mulled over the camper's manual trying to match circled numbers with written descriptions. "Here's one at the very northern tip of the Chesapeake Bay. It sounds okay." I read the information to him.

"Good! That's perfect. We should be able to make it by dark."

"You guys stop fighting back there. It's going to be a long ride. Settle down and take a nap or something!" I tried to take my own advice. But, I kept listening to truck-sounds hoping the wheel stayed in place. In my mind Dr. Wiley's ominous admonition haunted me.

It was turning dusk as the van wound its way through the trees to the campgrounds. The heat and humidity had risen steadily all day. Luckily, there were a few sites left. Like old pros we unpacked our gear and prepared our temporary home. Many hands made quick work of the chores. A supper of soup and leftover sandwiches put everyone in a happier frame of mind. Ronnie and the kids couldn't wait to explore the area. They were pleased with the wilderness atmosphere. The dense cover made a sanctuary for birds and squirrels.

The darkness brought mosquitoes in quantity. There was little respite from the heat. The boys spread out their sleeping bags in the back of the van and used them like mattresses. The girls finally stopped giggling and snuggled down under the canvas roof of the trailer. I found it hard to get comfortable in the narrow bunk but Ronnie was snoring as soon as his head hit the pillow.

The next morning I was awakened by the din of hundreds of birds chirping a hymn to the sun in unison. At last there was a cool breeze. It felt good to lie looking out into the tree tops, listening to this strange alarm clock.

After a breakfast of pancakes and bacon, Ronnie took the truck to look for ice. The boys decided to find the swimming hole and the girls stayed with me to clean up. Hours went by and Ronnie hadn't returned. I started to worry, feeling stranded and alone. I needed him to supervise the boys, wherever they were. What a relief to spot the red van chugging down the trail!

"Where have you been?" My frustration turned to anger.

"You won't believe what happened. I had a flat! I put on the spare and went to look for a gas station to get it fixed. I drove for miles before I found one open. I forgot today was Sunday. We're really out in the sticks."

I was relieved and annoyed at the same time. "Would you please go look for the boys? They went swimming hours ago and I haven't seen them since."

Trouble seemed to be following us. Was this some kind of omen? Maybe, we never should have come on this trip.

The campground turned out to be so enjoyable we stayed two days. The morning of the third day we packed up everything and started out determined to make it to the mountains by night-fall. As we traveled along the super-highways, through Baltimore and the outskirts of Washington, I kept hearing a funny noise coming from beneath the truck. Ronnie didn't seem to notice it. I began to get nervous. Every time he put on the brakes it would happen.

"What's that noise?" I asked casually wanting to keep quiet but afraid not to mention it.

"What noise?"

"That scraping sound when you step on the brakes."

"That? Oh, probably a branch got stuck underneath back at the campsite. It's nothing." Ronnie shrugged.

"What do you mean nothing. Don't you hear it?" I didn't like being put off.

"Oh, stop worrying."

That did it! I vowed not to say another word even if all four wheels fell off.

The noise followed us. It got louder and louder. The silence between Ronnie and me became deafening. Finally, Ronnie pulled over and looked under the truck.

"Are you satisfied? There's no stick," he said as he climbed back in.

"Then it must be something mechanical."

"I guess we should stop at a gas station and have it checked out."

"Ronnie, I just remembered, I have an old girl friend from high school who lives around Washington. I think in Rockville." I flipped through my pocket address book. "Maybe, we can drop in on her unexpectedly. When we stop for lunch I'll see if I can find her number in the telephone book. I don't seem to have it."

At the restaurant, I found Shirley's name and number and mustered the courage to dial her home. She was surprised and delighted to hear my voice. I was surprised to find she lived just a mile away and delighted when she invited us over.

While Ronnie took the van to a service station, Shirley, the kids and I spent the afternoon at the local swim club. I was thankful the children didn't have to hang around another hot, smelly garage and could cool off in a refreshing pool.

When we returned to the house, Ronnie explained how the brakes on the truck were so bad they were scraping bare metal and even the brake drums had to be replaced.

"Oh, it wasn't a stick?" I just had to rub it in. "Just suppose we had been in the mountains and the brakes gave way. That makes number three in close calls, all within three days."

"Somebody up there must like us," grinned Ronnie.

Shirley and her husband asked us to stay the night but everyone wanted to make it to the mountains. Besides, we had imposed long enough. We said our thank you's and goodbyes and left soon after supper.

"Blue Ridge Mountains here we come," said Ronnie happily.

"Yeah!" A cheer rose from the back of the van. Things were looking up. We rode through the early evening and into the summer night which never seemed to turn dark. As we climbed higher, the air grew cooler and smelled fresher. The children dozed. About 10 p.m. we pulled into a private campsite near the entrance to the park.

"Let's pack it in for the night. The kids are beat." Ronnie was beat, too.

Convinced our trials and tribulations were behind us, the next five days were spent exploring the Skyline Drive and enjoying one of the most beautiful parks in the United States. On the way home we visited Williamsburg, Virginia and continued north by way of the Chesapeake Bay Bridge and Tunnel. The ferry ride over the Delaware River was the high point of the whole trip and we returned tired but contented, the wanderlust satisfied for another year.

Medicine is the most distinguished of all the arts, but through the ignorance of those who practice it, and those who casually judge such practitioners, it is now of all the arts by far the least esteemed.

Hippocrates

8

The paper checkerboard

"I see you're back." Dr. Wiley seemed a little disappointed his dire predictions hadn't come true.

It was not without qualms I returned with Tim, as promised, to face the music at the clinic.

"Tim had a terrific time. We all did. Camping is good for the soul."

"But hard on the body," he quipped.

"Sometimes, the soul has priority."

"The soul needs a healthy body."

"We do the best we can with what we've got."

Wiley rifled the papers in his hand. "The tests show Tim's kidney function is very, very low," Wiley said getting down to the business of medicine.

"What can be done?"

"At the moment, nothing. Eventually, as his kidneys continue to deteriorate, I will put him on a low protein diet. But right now, since he seems to be operating normally, we won't do anything."

"After all that fuss I thought you would at least put him on some new medication or something," I zinged.

"We have to keep a close eye on his condition. You must bring him in for regular checkups." Wiley was quick to get on the defensive.

"Can he go to school as usual? Take gym?" I said not wishing to relinquish the ball.

"Of course. He can do anything he feels up to doing."

I could have told him that.

Wiley continued, "It's up to you how you handle it. Use your own judgement. I'm sure that's what you'll do anyway."

He was beginning to catch on.

The summer flew by and fall returned on schedule. Tim was in junior high school and loved to play touch football with his friends. I cringed inwardly when he talked about trying out for the school team in a few years but I kept quiet. I didn't want to squelch his hopes, not yet.

A paper route kept him busy and put some change in his pocket. Leo had the route before him and when he tired of it, Tim inherited it. There were about twenty-five customers but the houses were spread far apart in that section of town. He had to do a lot of walking, which I didn't think could hurt him. Sometimes, Leo would help but Tim didn't like splitting the profits. He preferred to do it alone. He was saving for a drum set.

Ronnie helped Tim deliver papers with the van whenever he could, especially on Sundays. We never mentioned to Tim that we thought he should slow down or take it easy. Sometimes, when he would complain of a backache, Ronnie would look at me with an unformed question in his eyes. We were both thinking the same thing.

One cold, rainy February evening, I returned from work to find Tim collapsed on the sofa.

"What's the matter, Tim?"

"My back is really killing me," he said. I felt his head. He wasn't warm enough for a fever.

"Did you get wet?"

"Yeah, soaked."

"Do you have any homework tonight?"

"Yeah, but I'm too tired. I delivered all my newspapers, though," he said with pride, "by myself!"

That foolish, spunky kid, I thought. What a supreme effort he must have made.

I called Dr. Wiley and the next morning I took him to the hospital for blood work and urine tests. By the time we got home, his temperature was over 102 degrees. The next day he slept so soundly he didn't hear the phone ring when I called to check on him from work. Lisa telephoned me when she got home from school.

"Tim is sound asleep on the sofa, right where he was when

we left this morning," Lisa reported.

"Wake him up and try to get him to eat some hot soup," I instructed.

About 4:30 while still at work, I called Wiley about the test results and Tim's condition.

"His chemistries show his calcium is low and his BUN (the urea and nitrogen levels in the blood) is very high. I'm afraid, Mrs. Fringuello, *he's near the end.*"

It suddenly flashed through me like a bolt of lightning what he was saying. *Tim was going to die.* They had been right, all those doctors, damn them. They said he would never live past puberty. I hadn't believed them, not really. Tim acted so normal, so healthy. He had fooled them all before. Why not now? I had prayed to God for a miracle, to let his kidneys be healed. If he had to die, why had he been spared so long? It wasn't fair. *God, don't turn your back on us now!*

The voice on the phone continued. "Bring him into the hospital tonight. We'll take chest x-rays immediately and check his vital signs every two hours. Is he lethargic?" The doctor's question brought me back to reality.

"Yes, I tried to call him at lunch time and he didn't answer. I don't think he heard the phone at all and he was sleeping right next to it."

"Lethargy is a sign of kidney failure. Get him in here as soon as possible."

My hands shook as I hung up the phone. Why did Wiley have to say, "he's near the end" so abruptly? Especially over the phone! It took all the guts out of me, a low blow. It paralyzed me to hear it said so heartlessly. Had the man no tact? Thank goodness it was almost quitting time. I couldn't concentrate now if my life depended on it! Why did I say, *my life?* It wasn't *my life*, it was *his life.* He was the one who was dying...or was it me? Everything spun around in my head. Would five o'clock never come?

The next few days were a seesaw. At first, Dr. Wiley put Tim on a special no-salt, no-protein diet that included lots of rice and potatoes. Tim acted very drowsy. He complained about a bad headache and that everything looked dark around the edges. It frightened him. They took blood tests and x-rays to see if there was any blockage of the urine. Then, Dr. Wiley reversed himself. He said Tim was now dehydrated and ordered an I.V. containing, of all things, salt water.

"I want him to drink large quantities of water. You can bring him potato chips and salty snacks."

"Oh, really? I thought he couldn't have salt."

"Well, I changed my mind," Wiley said. "He's putting out tremendous amounts of urine, much more than before. If he had a blockage, it was only temporary."

When Wiley left, I looked at the bottle that collected his urine. "Do you think you are producing more than usual?" I asked Tim.

"Nah, he doesn't know what he's talking about," said Tim.

Within a few days Tim was feeling better but just as we all began to breath a little easier, he took a turn for the worse. When Ronnie went to visit, he was surprised to find Tim back in bed. The nurse said he hadn't felt good all day. He'd complained of being drowsy and dizzy again. I called Dr. Wiley to find out why we hadn't been notified.

"My husband was in to see Tim tonight and he wasn't feeling so good. What's up?"

"Oh? He was fine at noon when I saw him."

"Tim says he's dizzy and won't get out of bed."

"Well, don't believe him. He's in good shape. His BUN is stabilizing."

"But, Ronnie said he is acting dopey again, and incoherent."

"If Tim's condition has worsened, I would have been notified immediately," Dr. Wiley insisted.

Wiley was getting on my nerves. He was like a cat jumping from one hot tin roof to another. He believed in the tests and only the tests, fully, explicitly. He wouldn't accept the obvious. Now I knew why doctors never ask patients how they feel; they never believe them. Medical chauvinism on the loose.

When I repeated my conversation to Ronnie, he was furious.

"That S.O.B! Is he calling me a liar? I tell you, Timmy doesn't feel right and I can see for myself he doesn't act right, either. Maybe Wiley didn't see him at all today. Him and his goddamn tests. He can take 'em and shove 'em."

The next day Tim had a puffy moon-face and very high blood pressure. The nurses admitted it was caused by the saline I.V. I couldn't get in touch with Wiley at all. It was his weekend off. Maybe it was just as well. My hostility was ready to burst the dam of civility.

That night I couldn't sleep. I kept picturing the hospital as a giant paper checkerboard. The doctors were the kings and queens. Timmy, Ronnie and I were the pawns. I wanted to take the whole set, crumple it into a ball and throw it out the window.

I didn't know how to play. I wanted to quit. I couldn't learn with an incompetent instructor who kept changing the rules.

When I went to visit Tim, he was very quiet.

"I brought your math book," I said brightly, trying to cheer him up. "Your teacher said to do from page 279 to 285."

Tim glanced at the pages I held open for him. "I can't do that. I don't understand it."

"I'll help you. We'll read the instructions together."

Tim took the book and flipped through the pages. "I'm going to get so far behind I'll never catch up. And that's just math. What about the other subjects?"

"When you get home, they're going to send you a tutor, right to the house. You'll do fine."

"But, I won't have time for my paper route. I'll never be able to save enough for a drum set." He threw himself back on the pillows and turned his head away. A few tears trickled down but he wiped them away quickly.

"And they gave me the wrong tray at dinner," he complained. "Just as I was ready to eat, they took it away and gave me this." He uncovered the half eaten dish of rice and noodles that were sitting on his night table. It didn't look very appetizing.

"You're not suppose to have any meat."

"They won't even let me have a banana."

"I guess it must have something in it your not supposed to have, either." I knew how he loved bananas.

"And you know, Mom," he said, almost in tears again, "they keep giving me too many potatoes. Potatoes at every meal."

"But, you like potatoes, don't you?"

"Yeah, but so many? I'm going to get fat."

I could see him smile a little, and then, I smiled. He was worried about getting fat?

"Seriously, Mom, if I keep eating potatoes and don't get any exercise, I will. So every morning I've been doing push-ups in bed."

That crazy kid. "I'll talk to Dr. Wiley about going home."

"He's a jerk."

"But he's the one who has to give permission."

Just as they thought they had his sodium balance straightened out, Tim's blood pressure shot up sky-high for no apparent reason. He frightened everyone. They still wouldn't let him go home, even after the medication brought it down. Another week of hemming and hawing went by. Tim was getting homesick. I reminded Wiley he had been in the hospital almost a month. Finally, he consented.

When I arrived to pick him up, Dr. Wiley and another doctor who I had never met, were waiting for me. We went into a small visitor's room to talk.

"Tim's kidney function has stabilized," Dr. Wiley began, "but because it is so low, you must keep him on a protein-free diet. I have discussed his case with the other urologist here at Presbyterian and we think he would be a good candidate for a kidney transplant."

"A transplant?" I said with surprise. "I was told years ago by doctors right here at this hospital that even if the procedure were perfected, Tim would never be eligible because of his other urinary problems. The danger of infection would be too great."

"Things have progressed since then," said Wiley. "Many ideas have changed. One advantage is his age. He's young. His heart is strong. Most important, he has the right attitude."

"You mean he's a fighter?" I thought of his push-ups in bed.

"Exactly. That's half the battle." There was a ring of admiration in his voice.

"And where will he get the kidney, from someone who has died?" I asked naively.

"Actually, in his case, the best donor would be someone related to him, like either you or your husband."

The words hit me like a bombshell. For some reason, even though I had wondered about transplants, it never entered my mind we might be asked to be donors. Suddenly, I felt as if I had had a cocktail too many. My tongue thickened. My vision blurred. Fear penetrated my being. I hardly heard the doctors' voices as they continued to present their case, smoothly, persuasively, quoting statistics and facts.

"The chances of him living three to five years with a transplant are 80%."

"Tim will need an additional operation."

"It's his only chance for survival."

"They'll check out his bladder to see if there is any possibility of returning him to normal."

"You and your husband will have blood tests to determine the best donor." Their voices faded in and out.

"If you want, we can take your blood sample right now."

I couldn't fight their high pressured tactics and without protest, I submitted to their needles. Perhaps this was how Dracula hypnotized his victims. I couldn't speak but my mind was racing. I could never let them take a kidney from Ronnie. I needed him too much. It would be just one more thing to worry about. Never in a million years would I ask someone else, family or no family. It all boiled down to me, I realized. I knew I'd be the perfect match. Why does it always have to be me, I thought. *Why do I have to do everything myself?*

I stood in front of a line of doctors. They were all there, every one of them, with their white coats and self-satisfied faces, every doctor who had ever had anything to do with Tim. I began to shout at them. I used all the curse words and obscenities I could think of. I shouted until I had no voice left. Then, I took a pin and pricked each one. I watched as the air sizzled out and there was nothing left but limp, wet balloons. I began to laugh, hysterically.

Still laughing, I realized it was all a dream. Is this what happens when you crack up, I wondered? The laughter dissolved into deep sobs. Ronnie sat up in bed with a start.

"What is it?"

"Just a bad dream," I sighed.

He rolled over and put his arm around my shoulder.

"It's okay. Don't cry." His unexpected tenderness made more tears come. He patted my back gently, comforting me like a baby. We laid in each others arms, his closeness soothing me. I drew upon his strength as a plant draws life-giving moisture from the earth. I needed him at that moment and my need was fulfilled. In an instant I knew why God had planned for man and woman to cling together as one; to sustain each other.

In a little while, I wiped my eyes. "I dreamed I was sticking pins in all the doctors."

He chuckled. "I hope you stuck a big one in Wiley Coyote."

"I couldn't see their faces but he was one of them. They were all there." A final sob wracked my body.

"What are you planning to do today?" Ronnie said tickling me with his unshaven chin.

"I have to go food shopping, it's Saturday, isn't it? And I suppose I should clean up around here. The place is a mess. Stop tickling me." I was getting annoyed.

"Well, at least you don't have to go to the hospital."

"Yeah, thank goodness. What are *you* planning to do this weekend besides work at the shop?

"Work on the lawn, probably. Tell Leo I want him to rake all those dead leaves in the back."

"I wish you'd fix the faucet upstairs. It's got a really bad drip now."

"I just fixed the damned thing." Ronnie swung his feet over

the side of the bed. Ever since Amy was born we'd been sleeping on the living room sofa. We gave the kids all three bedrooms upstairs. We had found room for five but lost our privacy. He pulled on his T-shirt. "C'mon, get up. I'll fix the coffee."

This was the best time of the day. The children were not up yet. Peace and quiet saturated the place. We cherished these few minutes together.

"I'm glad the little bugger is home," he said, nodding toward the ceiling.

"Did you see him eat last night? He acted starved to death. It's going to be hard to keep him on that diet."

"Be sure you find out where to get that special bread they told you about. What's it called, non-gluten?"

"Ummm. How are we ever going to remember to give him all those pills? There must be seven different kinds, a meal in itself."

"I guess you'll have to keep a chart. He can help keep track of it himself. What are they for?"

"Some are for his blood pressure. He gets very drowsy after he takes them. He's still getting cramps in his legs."

"When am I supposed to get the blood test taken?" asked Ronnie. "You know, to see if I can be the donor. Didn't they take yours already?"

"Yes, before we came home. Dr. Wiley said he would arrange for yours next week."

"Well, bug his ass."

In keeping with the plan, Dr. Wiley made an appointment for Ronnie to get the blood test early the next week.

"I'm here for the tissue-typing," Ronnie told the lab technician when he arrived at the hospital.

"Tissue-typing?" She acted startled.

"Yeah, you know, to see if I can be the donor for the kidney transplant you're going to do on my son, Timothy Fringuello."

"But tissue typing is an extremely complicated test. You have to have it done at the same time as your son, or at least within the same hour. It requires special preparation on our part. Even after we draw the blood samples, it takes seven hours to complete."

"Seven hours! My wife had it done a little while back. At least that's what Dr. Wiley told her."

"No, not tissue-typing," she said flipping through her records. "Nobody in your family has been tested."

"Now I'm sure Wiley is an idiot," Ronnie muttered under his breath.

"I can set up an appointment for the three of you later this week. How about Thursday at 7:30 a.m.?"

"Good! The sooner the better."

This time they were ready for us. Enormous vials of blood were drawn. One nurse gently rotated each test tube to prevent the blood from clotting. Tim didn't flinch as his arm was stuck. Blood tests were routine with him.

"You're next, Mr. Fringuello. Sit over here, please." The lab nurse was hardly old enough to be out of high school. Her stiff white dress, wooden clogs and blonde braids made her look like a little Dutch girl.

"Okay Dracula," Ronnie said trying to hide his nervousness. He continued to joke without really looking at what the nurse was doing with her instruments of torture until the end. Then, as the last vial was drawn, he gracefully slid off the chair in a dead faint. The pint-sized nurse reached out to grab his six-foot frame but she was unable to stop his steady progression downward. He glided neatly through her arms and onto the floor.

"I need help here," she called as two orderlies rushed to her side.

Timmy laughed his head off. "Hey, Dad. What happened? Did the light go out?" he teased with glee as Ronnie looked around, dazed.

The orderlies helped dear old Dad onto a stretcher.

"The whole room started going around," he said, embarrassed that he had made a spectacle of himself.

"Did you have any breakfast?" asked the nurse. She quickly took his blood pressure.

"Just coffee."

"We'll get you some orange juice. Stay put for a few minutes until we get some sugar into you. You'll be okay."

On the way home Timmy was still chuckling. It was the highlight of his day. Big strong Dad couldn't stand the sight of a little blood!

We learned immediately that we all had type "O" blood. The final results would take at least a week. Ronnie and I continued on pins and needles, waiting. He wanted to be the donor, badly. But there was something about Tim that resembled my side of the family. Maybe it was because Tim had always been chubby like Grandpop Anderson or because he had lighter skin and freckles like me. I was positive I would be the match.

The awareness both flattered and frightened me. To be chosen meant I would be taking part in the most important drama of my son's life. Tim and I would be the main actors of a life or death performance, the headline attraction. It would be only the fifth operation of its kind to take place at this hospital. Other hospitals, large teaching hospitals, had done several. But here it was only the beginning of a transplant program. I could imagine Wiley as Boris Karloff rubbing his hands together excitedly in anticipation of a "very interesting case."

Beneath the excitement lay frightening questions. Would it be successful or would it all amount to nothing? Would giving up my kidney shorten my own life or hamper it in any way? Would I have the courage to go through with it, to face the pain? Were we all just part of an experiment?

Finally, the telephone call came. I was informed that the test were completed but there had not been a suitable match. While we all had type "O" blood, Ronnie and I had Rh positive and Tim had Rh negative.

Neither of us would make suitable donors!

THE SYCAMORE TREE

Here beneath the sycamore tree, I sit
*   and gaze with longing at the wondrous*
*   world around me;*
There are rich, ripe fruits to be gathered.

I watch intently as the workers pluck
*   the luscious grapes from the vineyards*
*   and the farmer gathers his grain from the fields;*
I must reach out and join in the harvest,
*   There is so much to be done and so little time.*

What pure joy to taste the sweet sweat
*   of labor on my lips,*
What deep satisfaction I find
*   in the rhythmic movements of my physical being,*
And when the day has been fulfilled,
*   I lie down to peaceful dreams.*

The sycamore spreads its branches,
*   The bounty lays unclaimed;*
I cannot join the race,
*   My body withers into useless dust.*

J. Fringuello

9

'The long hill down

The reality of the situation set in along with a deep depression. The only thing that could save Timothy now was hemodialysis, a mechanical method of purifying the blood. Life on a machine was limiting and limited.

Over the years I had read how kidney dialysis could extend the lives of patients with complete kidney failure. Its invention was welcomed as a tremendous breakthrough for science. Man at last had the power to postpone the inevitable, *death.*

I considered it with dread. Would I be asked to operate a machine for the sake of my child's life? The responsibility seemed so frightening I pushed it out of my mind and refused to think about it. I wanted to be a good mother but did mothering necessarily include monitoring a machine for countless hours?

Mothering was supposed to be warm and human, not manipulating a cold heartless machine. I would be a slave chained to an impossible task like the princess in the fairy tale who spun straw into gold. The more she spun the more straw she was given.

To give up my time on a regular basis would be giving up a precious part of me. I would suffocate. I would hate every second of it and I would become a miserable, ill-tempered martyr. I despised martyrs. Everyone despised them.

In despair, I wrote in my journal:

Now there is no hope. A machine will dominate his life and our whole family life will revolve around it. It's the last straw. I don't know if I can live with this. Ever since I can remember I've fought to control my life. I've been headstrong, willful, determined to overcome every obstacle that was thrown in my path. How can I accept defeat? Life will have no meaning. He's a fighter, too. How will he be able to accept this? Is there freedom only in death? The trap of life is closing...

It was late March and spring had begun to stir the earliest bulbs. Green shoots began to push through the ground cover of dead leaves. Buds on the trees and bushes were swelling to the bursting point. I looked upon the season with eyes glazed with grief. New life only reminded me of my son's impending death. Tears filled my eyes and came tumbling down without being coaxed. There was no bottom to my well of despair as it overflowed in a continuous stream.

In the past, spring had meant delightful exercise raking away old leaves, preparing flower beds, keeping a watchful eye over the opening buds. This year I was immobile, unable to lift a finger. I could barely exert enough effort to do the household chores.

I managed to get through work every day. The familiar routine kept me from becoming catatonic. I was trying to keep the truth from my employer, afraid she might use this as an excuse to fire me, and I needed the job. I put up a cheerful exterior and did not discuss it with anyone except Emily, a co-worker and fellow artist. She faced a similar circumstance; her mother was dying of cancer. Her ironic sense of humor gave balance to our situations. As we struggled to please our demanding employer by drawing smiling animals for grade school book catalogs, we weighed the trivial against the traumatic.

I was a sporadic church-goer at best and now I stopped going altogether. There was no one there I felt particularly close to. When you meet someone casually at Sunday services and she says, "How are you, how's the family?" what do you answer? How can you capsulize everything that has been happening into two short sentences? And if you could, who would want to hear it? Should I say, "Hello, I'm fine but my son is dying of kidney failure?" What's the point of trying to explain. It takes too much energy. I even avoided the pastors, well meaning as they were.

One minister was so young I knew he couldn't possibly understand my problem and the other was so old I couldn't relate to him either. The last thing I wanted was to hear platitudes about God's infinite wisdom. Going to church made me uncomfortable.

My best friend had moved about 40 miles away and she seemed to avoid contacting me. I guess she just didn't know what to say. Her apparent lack of interest in my problem and what I perceived as a lack of empathy from others made me withdraw even more.

Even my parents' attitude annoyed me. At times, when I felt like talking, I would phone my mother but hold back on the really bad stuff. I always had a hard time expressing myself to her. Sometimes I did try, but whenever I would start to lean a little she would make it clear I should take care of my own problems. My father always protected her with guilt-provoking words like, "Don't upset your mother, it's her heart, you know." In all fairness to them, they were very independent individuals, never asking for help from us and therefore expecting not to be asked in return. They had had plenty of heartaches in their life over the years so why should I burden them with mine now?

My closest friend and confidant was my husband, Ronnie. Only he truly understood. He masked his own feelings of disappointment and became my strong arm of support. He pitched in whenever he saw me faltering. He coaxed, persuaded and threatened the kids into caring for the house. The tenderness he showed me can never be described in words. It deepened our love for each other and kept me sane.

Tim and I went weekly to Dr. Wiley's office. The doctor tried to cheer me with encouraging words about Tim.

"He's holding his own nicely."

"Is he?"

"Yes his blood pressure isn't fluctuating as much. He can start back to school on a half-day schedule."

"But he has difficulty staying awake. How can he go to school? He has no energy at all."

"The school should be able to provide transportation for him. He won't have to take gym. I think he can learn to live with it."

"Live with it?" I angrily raised my voice. "You try living with it. I can't!" I began to cry. He didn't understand the weight of the problem at all, the weight that seemed to rest on my shoulders, alone. I wanted to run away from the whole mess. I wanted to jump on the nearest plane to some tropical paradise where there would be no more worry, no pain. The doctor was trying to be sympathetic but to me his pity seemed empty and phony.

"Look, it's not the end of the world. Tim may not be able to use your kidney, or your husband's, but we can put him on the cadaver list. He may get a match from a perfect stranger. The only problem is, he'll have to wait until one is available."

"It's the waiting that's killing me, the not knowing what's going to happen. I'm a very impatient person."

"Tim is doing very well, under the circumstances. Compared to other children with this problem, he's doing fantastic."

I didn't believe him. Before we left I decided to put into effect a plan I had been forming in my mind.

"Doctor, I haven't been sleeping well lately. Do you think you could give me something to help me sleep?" I lied.

"Ah, well, yes, I guess I can give you something." He pulled out a prescription pad and scribbled on it.

"Here, try this. Let me know how it works."

I stuffed the paper guiltily into my purse. It was my passport. I had the prescription filled and placed the bottle high up in the closet where no one would notice. Sometimes, when I felt I would never make it through the day, I would open the closet door and stare up at the bottle. It gave me a peculiar feeling of security to know it was there. Then, before anyone came near, I would close the door quickly. It was my little secret. My red button of destruction.

An unexpected glimmer of hope appeared on the horizon. The hospital called. It was Miss Plummer.

"We'd like to redo the tissue-typing test. This time we will send it to a lab in California."

"Do you think there is still a chance one of us might be a donor?"

"Well, the West Coast is more experienced with this kind of testing. We're trying to cover every possibility. Can you all come in again, say, Monday morning?"

Incurable optimism crept over me, but with reservations.

"Yes," I said, "of course, we'll be there."

Again we trooped into the city to an expectant Dracula and again we waited for the results, this time much longer. We were betting heavily this time, the whole wad, and when the results came in, we had a winner. *And I was it!*

There was no doubt in my mind now. I would do it. I had to. I had seen the alternative, the dark side. I had experienced despair. I had no choice.

While I was selfishly struggling for sanity, Tim was struggling to live. He tackled each day with calm persistence. His stubborn determination shamed me in my self-pity. This terrible thing was happening to *Tim*, not to *me*. He was the victim, the one who was dying. I had been trying to die for him. It wasn't I who would go on dialysis. I had been wallowing in my own self-centeredness. As I faced the truth, the black cloud began to lift ever so slightly. For me, it was the turning point. But just in case, the bottle of sleeping pills remained snug and untouched in the closet, always ready for my quick getaway.

With the question answered as to who the donor would be, it now became evident it was just a matter of time before the transplant could take place. Or so I thought. The doctors said Tim wasn't ready yet. His kidneys were still functioning slightly. They couldn't go ahead until he had complete renal shutdown.

Ronnie and I evaluated the situation.

"Dr. Wiley thinks he should go back to school. I don't see how he can get through even half-days. He's really dragging."

"What's making him so dopey?"

"I guess it's the blood pressure medication. He gets dizzy and can't focus his eyes."

"Well, suppose you don't give him so many?"

"His blood pressure may go way up again."

"Maybe, and maybe not. Wiley's just going by educated guesses."

"If I had a blood pressure gage I could keep track of it. What are they called?"

"Some crazy name like sphagmomanometer."

"Can anyone buy them, I wonder?"

"I don't know. Try a surgical supply store. There's one near us I think."

It was as if the two of us had formed an alliance. Our common sense and love for Tim against the impersonal, machine-like workings of medical men. We weren't trying to prove we were superior. We just wanted to make some logical moves that would let things proceed comfortably for everyone, addressing the little things overlooked by the professionals. Henceforth, we would take every bit of information offered, examine it critically and decide if, when and how to apply it to Tim's case.

I located a place to purchase the blood pressure cuff and practiced taking Tim's pressure. I discontinued giving him one dosage of blue pills. It helped a little and his blood pressure stayed fairly steady. He began school and with great effort tried to fit back into the educational system. A taxi picked him up three days a week.

"Ronnie, he's still very listless. What do you think would happen if he began to eat more meat?" It had been a week since he started back to school. "I know he misses it. One ounce a day is nothing. It's almost as if his body craves it, like it needs more protein to sustain itself. He is a growing boy."

"His body is trying hard to grow but I don't think it's succeeding."

"Suppose we try it for a week? Let him eat whatever he wants and see what happens."

"It's better than sitting here doing nothing."

For one week we let him eat. What a difference! He perked right up. The body that was struggling so hard to function began to take on some of its old characteristics. It made us feel good to watch him eat. He enjoyed it so much.

A week later, after Tim's routine blood tests, Dr. Wiley called me on the phone.

"I don't understand it. Your son's BUN has gone up from 38 to 74. Is there anything the matter?"

"I have to confess, we let him eat more protein than usual."

"You can't let him do that, Mrs. Fringuello. It throws his chemistries all out of whack."

"But, mentally, he's a changed person. He's not moping around anymore. He's actually enjoying life a little. Don't you think because of his age, because his body is trying to grow, that he needs extra energy? He's sick of rice and potatoes."

"Absolutely not! He will go into uremia much faster if you let him do that!"

Chastised, I hung up the phone. Maybe it wasn't such a bad idea to speed things up. I wondered what he would do if it was his son. Would he go by the book so precisely? Is medicine a science, truly, or an art?

"We can't let him eat meat," I told my husband that night. "His BUN went skyhigh."

"But he acts so much better."

"I know but if he keeps it up he'll build up poisons his body can't throw off. And then he'll go into uremia."

"He *acts* better," Ronnie insisted.

"Let's be logical about this. We'll cut back on the protein but not so drastically."

"He's going to be disappointed."

We called Tim and explained what had happened. We always

told him the truth. A simplified version, but the truth.

"I'm still putting out urine," he said hopefully.

"But the kidneys are not doing their job. All the poisons are not being flushed out with the water."

It was a letdown but as usual he accepted it. "I thought maybe I could start playing ball again if I had more energy," he said wistfully.

My husband and I exchanged glances. I wanted to tear my heart out. An ordinary little boy's dream went up in smoke and there was nothing we could do. It was so hard to sit by and watch.

"After you get your new kidney from Mom, you'll have lots of energy," Ronnie explained. "For now, we just have to be patient and take it slow."

After Tim left, Ronnie growled, "I wish they would start the ball rolling. This waiting is for the birds."

"I have an appointment to see Dr. Lambro next week. He's one of the big wheels, according to Wiley. The decision will be up to him."

"I hope he's got a few brains," grumbled Ronnie.

Dr. Lambro was late for our 5:30 appointment. As he introduced himself, I realized he did not live up to my expectations of a doctor. He was of average height, slim and younger than I. There was a ruggedness to his features and yet the smallness of his bone structure gave a sensitive impression. The most conspicuous thing about him was his hair. It was sandy colored, very curly and rather long, giving the effect of a cross between a little boy and a seedy professor. It seemed in need of grooming partly because he was constantly running his fingers through it and partly because it grew that way naturally.

He wore the customary white doctor's jacket opened carelessly over his corduroy slacks. His tie was knotted loosely in a token gesture of conformity and cocked at an angle where he had jerked it, unconsciously.

Another characteristic which was not apparent at first was his voice. Controlled and well-modulated, its tone inspired confidence. It was masculine without being overbearing. He was easy to talk to because he did not assume the traditional role of "me doctor, you patient." There was no attempt on his part to convince me of his importance. Rather, he went to the opposite extreme of purposeful humility without sounding insincere.

When he arrived he had his three children with him, their

ages about five, four and two. The youngest had the curliest mass of brilliant red hair I have ever seen, as unruly as his father's. At first I was a little annoyed that we would not be able to talk in private but he patiently settled the children in an adjoining office with papers and pencils and the only interruption was the passing of notes under the door printed in childish scrawl, "I love you Daddy."

"I haven't met your son yet but Dr. Wiley says he's quite a boy," Dr. Lambro began.

"Oh, did you hear about his push-ups in bed?"

"Yes, it's amazing how well adjusted he is after all he's been through. You've done a good job with him."

"I can't take any credit for that. I did what I had to do. I couldn't have done it any other way."

"What do you mean?"

"It would have been next to impossible to hold him back. He always insisted on keeping up with his brother. To be fair, we let him and to tell the truth, it was easier."

"His attitude makes him a candidate for our dialysis-transplantation program. You know, he wouldn't be chosen unless he had you as the available donor. The fact there are other children in the family also is in his favor." His voice was firm and matter-of-fact but I tensed, waiting for the pitch.

"You mean, in case he needs another donor in the future?"

"Exactly."

"I guess I should be grateful he has been picked." For some reason at that moment I resented that I was expected to feel grateful. Like a battle-shocked soldier I wondered why we had been saved and yet I felt I was being manipulated into this position.

"There are many others who die."

I burned with thanklessness. I refused to feel indebted. He needs us as much as we need him, I thought to myself. Shut up and don't make waves.

"Will he have to go on the dialysis machine?" I asked, mentioning the very thing I was hoping to avoid.

"Yes, he will. Tim needs another operation before the transplant. The ileostomy will have to be moved to the other side to make room for the transplanted kidney. You see, the kidney is not put in the usual place, under the ribs. It's too inaccessible there. We want to put it in the lower abdomen where it can be removed easily if necessary."

"If it rejects, what happens?"

"We take it out, he goes on dialysis and he waits for a cadaver kidney."

"If it takes, how long will it last?"

"Statistics are changing all the time. It is a relatively new procedure as you know. Right now about 50% of them last five years."

"Five years! That's all?" My hopes plummeted. "It's not worth it. That's not long enough. Such sacrifice for just five years?" Self-pity engulfed me once again.

"But in five years who knows what may be discovered. So we give him your kidney, it lasts five years and it fails. Then we give him another, and so on." He made it sound routinely easy.

"Inconceivable! That may sound fine from a medical point of view but that's not leading a normal life. That's dying over and over, a thousand deaths. I'd rather be dead than have that hanging over my head." Funny, I thought, why did I say *I'd* rather be dead?

"I'm sorry you feel that way."

I didn't want to be felt sorry for. "I'm only human." I could feel my frustration growing. "What are the risks on my part?" I asked shifting the subject to me.

"Have you ever had major surgery before?"

I shook my head in the negative.

"You're lucky. You have to understand we will make a long incision in your lower back and around your rib cage to the front. We will remove a rib which may or may not grow back. Of course, you can expect pain right after the operation and you'll be quite sore for a while. In about two weeks you should be completely recovered.

"Before surgery, we will do a series of tests to see what kind of shape you're in and to decide which kidney is the best one to take. Sometimes we discover things the donor never expected, like for instance, one person had only one kidney functioning and he felt fine. Of course that made him ineligible, as was another person with three kidneys."

"What if I think there may be something else wrong with me?"

"Like what, for instance?"

"I've had some digestive problems, lately. I think there may be something wrong with my gall bladder or intestines."

"We'll check you out with a complete G.I. series."

"I see."

"Why haven't you had it checked out before?"

I shrugged. He thought I was looking for an excuse to back out. Maybe I was.

"Is there any possibility I will run into any problems as I grow older?"

"Of course, there's a chance but the odds of that happening are extremely slim. The average healthy person uses a very small part of his kidneys. He doesn't really need two. Since Tim didn't have a hereditary disease there's no need for you to worry about that at all." Dr Lambro's mannerism was definitely soft-sell. He was presenting his case in the best possible light and I was falling for it.

"Do you have any literature about transplantation I can read?"

"No, there has been nothing published for the layman."

"Nothing at all?" I found that hard to believe.

"No, I'm sorry."

Maybe some of his communication skills were modern but he still believed in keeping the patient as ignorant as possible.

That night as I lay in bed thinking about our conversation, the only thing I could clearly remember about Dr. Lambro was his voice. It was a reassuring voice. He seemed sincere and I wanted to put my full confidence in him yet there was a nagging feeling that I was being skillfully manipulated into making the right decision, the decision that was right for them.

In my half-sleep I pictured myself in a race, a marathon. It was the most important race of my life. I didn't dare trip or fall. There were hurdles on the track. I could see them and I knew with effort I could clear them. As I approached the first one I felt my adrenaline pumping. I started to make the leap when all of a sudden the hurdle was gone. Someone had moved it farther down the track, a dirty trick. I stumbled but did not fall. No rest for me, I must keep running. Didn't they know I was only a sprinter and not a marathon runner? I kept trying to wake up. I wished it was only a dream but the dream was real. There was a long course to run before the hurdle of transplantation.

Next, Tim must be prepared for dialysis.

APRIL

April, sweet April,
Thou maiden frail and fair,
Thou sprite whose lovely, dancing form
Is here, now everywhere;
Breathe thy warm, life-giving breath
Upon my wintery cheek,
Whisper to my longing ear,
And I will hear thee speak.

Sunlight saturates thy locks
Entwined with daffodils.
Then, drips in golden droplets
Upon the greening hills.
Thy earthy perfume haunts my rest
And lingers in the gloom,
What dire enchantment canst thou cast
That draws me from my room?

I stand with face uplifted,
I feel no hurt, no pain,
Ah, April my sweet April,
Thy tears fall as spring rain.

J. Fringuello

10

Pray for us sinners

The dialysis-transplant program was set up a few blocks away from the main hospital at Wakefield City Hospital. It was never explained to us clearly why it was arranged in this way but we were led to believe it had to do with State funding to city hospitals, all very hush-hush. We were assured, almost apologetically, that the unit would be staffed by competent nurses and doctors from the clinic.

The moment we walked into Wakefield we sensed a difference. The hustle and bustle of the large teaching hospital was missing. It was not as cheerful as the familiar Pediatric floor we were used to. It appeared relatively clean but in need of sprucing up. There was a cafeteria-like odor lingering in the hallways unsuccessfully disguised by disinfectant. It was hard to pinpoint but there was something second-class about this hospital.

As soon as school was finished in June, Tim was admitted to Wakefield. He didn't want to go. It was as if we were playing a dirty trick on him, from one prison to another.

"Tim's not ready for dialysis," said Dr. Lambro examining his tests and x-rays. "In preparation for it, however, we will put a shunt in his arm. This is a simple operation. We make an incision at the wrist and sew an artery into the vein. The artery pumps blood into the vein making it become engorged with blood. The vein will be the site of the needles used on dialysis. There is less chance of a vein collapsing."

"Will the shunt be visible from the outside?" I had seen another child's shunt. He was much smaller than Tim. A loop of plastic protruded from his forearm.

"Not really. His vein will eventually become larger in that arm which will be noticeable but there will be no plastic tubing sticking out. The advantage to the exterior shunt is the child does not have to be stuck with needles each time he is treated and there is no danger of the vein collapsing which can be a problem in a small child. The disadvantages are the arm can't get wet, special care must be taken when bathing, no swimming is allowed, blood clots may form in the tube and if the tube is accidentally pulled out, the child could bleed to death within a few minutes, a constant worry in an active child."

In one respect I was relieved. Bleeding to death was a fear I instantly recognized. But I felt sorry for Tim. Those needles were huge!

Events began to gain momentum. On July 3rd Tim went on dialysis for the first time. All the nurses made a big fuss over how well he did. Dialysis did not seem quite as bad to me as long as someone else accepted the responsibility of running the machine. And it is only temporary, I reasoned. If he can accept it, I can accept it.

At home, I was preparing the children to leave. Lisa, Donna and Amy were going for an extended stay with Grandma Anderson. She and Grandpop had offered to care for them at their seashore home. During this time of upheaval, I was thankful for their generous help.

Leo was spending six weeks at a combination summer school and camp in South Jersey. He had to make up a math course he'd failed during the school year. We had been so preoccupied with Tim, we'd slacked off in keeping an eye on the other's grades. His average was a "67" instead of the passing grade of "68". I felt it was a gross injustice but unable to find the time or energy to pursue the issue, we settled for summer school. With financial aid from my parents, we enrolled him in a boy's naval camp where he would receive the best supervision. Leo was sure we were shipping him off because we didn't love him. I was sorry he felt that way but under the circumstances we had no choice. I pushed his needs out of my mind and concentrated on Tim. I think Leo never forgave me for it.

On Saturday, July 4th, Ronnie drove the girls to Grandma's and Leo to camp. It was a cool, rainy day. Afraid he would run into shore traffic, Ronnie left at 5 a.m. They went out to breakfast at a pancake house when they got to the shore.

Grandma Fringuello and I went to visit Timmy. He was miserable. He had a throat infection and it was hard for him to swallow. Grandma brought him some fresh fruit hoping it would encourage him to eat, but it only made him worse. Because it was a holiday the staff was reduced to a few nurses and there was no doctor in sight.

On Sunday, Tim was worse. He began throwing up everything. I was impressed when Dr. Lambro himself came to take blood tests.

"Let's see if we can find a vein, Tim," the doctor said as he started poking him with the needle.

"We'll wait outside, Tim. Come on, Mama." I had to get outside before I started to scream at him. "I hope his surgical skills are better than his nursing ones," I mumbled to her. "Drawing blood is not one of his finest techniques."

In a few minutes Lambro joined us and took me aside. "I think Tim's kidneys have finally given out. We'll put him on dialysis again tomorrow."

"Isn't there anything you can do for him right now? He can't keep anything down."

"I've ordered a special enema called a potassium exchange. As a person goes into uremia the body finds it hard to get rid of potassium. Even dialysis can't flush it out. Hopefully it will help him to rest more comfortably.

"I'll have Miss Plummer from the unit keep an eye on him. She's just up the hall. She'll call me if there are any problems. Also, you can depend on Miss Brown, the head nurse on this floor." He started to leave.

"Oh, Dr. Lambro, I'm checking into the hospital tomorrow for the tests we discussed, the G.I. series and stuff."

"Good, we'll be expecting you." He hurried down the hall.

Miss Brown was a black angel of mercy. Why she was still a "miss" I'll never know. She fussed over Tim with parental concern and she made the other nurses aware of how special he was. One day as I went to gather up his dirty clothes to take home to wash, I couldn't find his underwear. "What happened to your clothes?" I asked Tim, thinking they had been stolen.

"Oh, don't worry, Miss Brown washed them for me."

Monday morning I got up early to get everything organized. I had taken vacation time from work to have the tests done. I had not told my employer the real problem yet. I'd be in the hospital about five days. Just as I was about to leave, Tim called on the phone.

"Hi, Mom?" He sounded chipper.

"Hello, Tim. What's the matter?"

"They just stuck me with the needles and I want you to bring in some ice pops, the cherry kind. The nurse says I can have them while I'm on dialysis."

"Are you sure?" I was pleased he felt like eating again. It was a good sign.

"Yes, Miss Plummer said I can eat things I can't have other times when I'm on the machine."

"Okay I'll bring in ice pops."

By the time I arrived at the hospital, he was loaded down with pops. Miss Brown had gone out for some and the kitchen had sent up more. The refrigerator was bursting. Everyone was eating ice pops, patients and nurses alike.

Admittance to Wakefield Hospital that morning was like entering a monastery. My preliminary testing as a donor was to take five days. After filling out the usual forms, my watch, wedding ring, jewelry, car keys and money were taken away for "safe keeping". Then, I was told to remove all my clothes and put on a stiff muslin gown and rough striped robe, two sizes too big, gathered at the waist with a cord. My street clothes were locked up. Stripped of all my worldly possessions, I was led, humbly, through the hall and up the main elevator to the 3rd floor. Where were they taking me, I wondered, to get my head shaved? No, my penance was to be seven enemas in five days, a thorough cleansing from the inside out. *Hail Mary!*

I shared a room with three other ladies and a bathroom with the whole floor. At the other end of the hall was dialysis. I could visit Tim any time I wanted. When the nurse announced proudly the purpose of my visit to my roommates, an old African-American lady at the end of the room threw up her hands and joyfully exclaimed, "Saints be praised. You're a wonderful woman. God bless you, bless you." *Blessed art thou amongst women.*

She continued to embarrass me by quoting phrases from the Bible. "And He lay down his life for his sheep," and "No greater love hath any man than this," and so on. These words, instead of comforting me, only made me more nervous. I was an imposter. I was living a lie. I had no intention of laying down my life like a martyr. I wasn't the loving, generous person envisioned by this kind soul. I was doing this because there was no other way out, because I had no choice. I despised myself for being a hypocrite. *Holy Mary, pray for us sinners.*

Later that afternoon, having finished my tests for the day, I was relaxing on the bed with a book, when suddenly two doctors ran past the door. I recalled what Ronnie had said about doctors running when someone died. I felt uneasy. I slid off the bed and followed them down the hall toward the dialysis unit. The nurse at the station saw me coming and casually closed the door to the unit. A Spanish-speaking man with a broom was intent on sweeping the hall.

"Why were the doctor's running?" I asked hoping this information source was a wise one.

"I don't know," he replied shrugging his shoulders and taking the opportunity to lean on his broom handle and contemplate. I walked slowly back up the hall and stood in the doorway of my room. *Pray for us sinners now and at the hour of our death!*

Another intern rushed into dialysis with a tank of oxygen on wheels. Blood rushed to my head. There were four patients in that room and one of them was my son. *Blessed is the fruit of thy womb, Jesus!*

A few minutes later, a dialysis nurse came up to me and took my sweating hand, sympathetically.

"Your son is all right," she said.

"What happened?" A sob caught in my throat.

"I'm not sure. I'll get a doctor to explain."

She brought back Dr. Lambro. I trembled as he spoke. *Forgive me Father for I have sinned.*

"Your son has had a seizure."

"What's a seizure?"

"A fit."

"What kind of fit?"

"An epileptic fit, as he was coming off dialysis. He hit his mouth on the arm rail of the bed and loosened a tooth. Nothing to worry about."

"I want to see him."

As I walked into the room, a hush fell. High voltage tension seemed to flash between those in attendance. Their eyes averted, everyone became very, very busy.

"What's the matter with you?" I asked Tim bluntly, loud enough for all to hear.

Bewildered, Tim shrugged and grimaced. I didn't know what else to say. I had to say something. They were all waiting.

"That's what we need, more dentist bills. We've already

spent over two hundred dollars on your brother."

There! Now everyone could take their second breath. What were they expecting, that I should scream negligence? Inside, my anger knuckled white against my skull. Questions screamed for answers. Why hadn't there been oxygen in the room? How long had he been unconscious? Who was to blame? Maybe I should have made a scene, but they were all as frightened as I was. They knew they were to blame. I could slice the guilt with a knife it was so thick. There was no point in prolonging the punishment. This crisis was over. *Mary, full of grace. The Lord is with thee. Amen.*

When they were sure he had recovered fully, they brought him back to his room. It was late. Dr. Lambro and the rest of the dialysis staff had gone home. Suddenly, Tim began to retch. This time a blackish-brown fluid. Even though his stomach was empty he continued to have violent attacks of dry heaves.

I went to find Miss Brown but the day shift had gone home hours ago. The nurse in charge tried to brush me off. When I requested she call the doctor on duty, she was full of excuses. I was suspicious of her reasons for not being able to reach him.

"I want to see the resident in charge."

"He's busy now."

"My son is throwing up. It's an emergency."

"I'm in charge here. Don't you go tellin' me when to call the doctor. I'll decide that."

Ronnie arrived about 6 p.m. I told him about Tim and the *episode.*

"And the head nurse refuses to call the doctor for him. I feel like she's laughing at us. She's nothing like Miss Brown. She's a real bitch. What shall we do? I feel so helpless without a phone."

"If she won't call the resident, I'll find a pay phone and call Lambro. What's his number?"

"Here, this is the answering service's number. I hope you can get through to him."

"Maybe I better go home to put in the call because when he calls back I don't want to be on a pay phone."

"Please hurry. He can't sleep. He's in agony."

"I'll tell Lambro if he doesn't get over here soon there won't be a patient to transplant."

I knew it was urgent that Ronnie contact Lambro but I hated for him to leave us in this hostile atmosphere. The nurse kept trying to chase me out of Tim's room.

"You can't stay here all night. Get back to your own room,"

she snapped.

"But visiting hours aren't over yet."

"Well, you ain't a visitor. You're a patient and patients need their rest."

"I'm waiting for the doctor."

"I tole you he's busy, with an emergency."

"But that was hours ago."

"You get on now. I got other patients to take care of. Your son ain't the only one."

What I was experiencing was a growing rift between the specially trained dialysis staff, who were primarily white, and the regular black staff at Wakefield.

Later that night, after receiving Ronnie's call, Dr. Lambro made a special trip into the hospital to give Tim injections to stop the vomiting.

Thank you God, I prayed. At last I have found someone I can trust. There's at least one doctor who cares.

By Friday my tests were completed and the floor doctor said I could go home...after one more enema.

They were stalling.

I looked in on Tim and there was an unfamiliar doctor sitting on the edge of his bed talking to him.

"Who was that?" I asked after he was gone.

"Dr, Wiesenfeld," said Tim.

"Isn't he the psychiatrist?"

"Yeah, I guess so." He wasn't impressed. "He asked me a lot of stupid questions."

"Did you answer them?"

"Some of them."

"You don't have to if you don't feel like it."

"I know."

So that was why they were slow to discharge me. They wanted me to talk the the psychiatrist, also. But why didn't they come right out and say it? Why were they being so sneaky about it?

Dr. Wiesenfeld was trained in traditional forms of psychiatric treatment, a real honest-to-goodness shrink.

Connected to the staff primarily for the purpose of research, his findings were confidential. If he felt there was a problem that could be solved, he was free to bring it up for consideration by the "team". My impression was the other doctors felt he was more of a nuisance than a necessity. He asked if I'd mind talking to him and we went into an unused private room.

I was on the defensive from the beginning.

"What annoys me about this psychoanalyst bit is, that it's a cop-out."

"What do you mean, cop-out?"

"Well, it's as if one doctor takes care of the kidneys, one takes care of the urinary tract and after the patient has been stuck full of needles and yells, 'Ouch!', they wonder, 'Whatever can be the matter with so and so? Call the psychiatrist. Let him find out what's troubling him'."

"Yes, more unity is needed between the team members," Dr. Wiesenfeld said, peering through his glasses. "Getting the other doctors to recognize the emotions of the patient is a problem I am interested in researching."

"I'm doing my own research. I'm keeping a diary of all this."

"Really?" His eyebrows almost jumped off his forehead. "How remarkable. I'd like to read it sometime."

"Maybe, when I'm ready. It's very personal." And become a statistic? Not on your life, I thought.

"How would you describe the situation you're in?" he asked.

I was ready for this one. "It's as if I were being pursued by a band of wild Indians."

"Oh?"

"They've chased me to the edge of the cliff. There's a river below. I know I'll have to jump into the river but I'm afraid I can't swim."

"Yes, and then what happens?"

"I'm going to jump but not until *I* get good and ready. I don't want to be pushed."

"Ummm... a very good analogy. It helps me understand what you are feeling." He wrote intently in his little black notebook.

"How do you feel about Tim?" It was my turn to ask questions.

"I think he has enormous trust."

"Really?" I wondered what Tim had said to make him come to that conclusion. "Trust in whom?"

"In the doctors, the nurses...everyone. These indians that are pursuing you, are you afraid of them?" We were back to me, again.

"Yes and no. I just feel I have to fight them."

"Are you afraid of the future?"

"No, I don't really think of that at all."

"What are you afraid of then?"

I thought for a few minutes. What *was* I afraid of? "Pain, I guess. The pain of the operation. The inconvenience. The medical expense. Of not being in control of the situation."

"You're used to being in control, aren't you. As a mother, what is it like not being in control of you son?"

His male smugness made the feminist part of me bristle. "I'm not 'just a mother', you know. I run an art department in a publishing firm. Talking about control, are you aware of the procedure for admittance here? They take away everything you own and lock it up. My clothes, my wedding ring, my money, even my car keys. What is this, an asylum for the criminally insane?"

"Really? I didn't know this. I'll mention it to the administration."

"You should. It's humiliating. Most hospitals in this day and age don't treat their patients like that." It felt good to put someone else on the spot.

"It's a pleasure talking to you, Mrs. Fringuello." Dr. Wiesenfeld was very punctual about his interviews. "If you want to talk to me in the future, here's my number."

I looked at his card. It had a Park Avenue address.

My clothes were returned along with a big brown envelope containing my personal items. The cold metal of the car keys felt good as I grasped them eagerly. This worldly sinner would never make a monk!

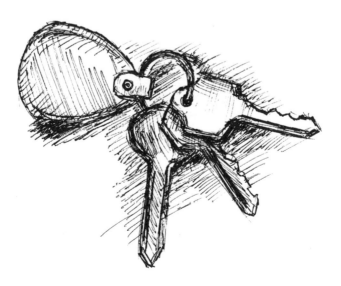

But Lord,
Be merciful to me, a fool!

Edward Rowland Sill

from

A Fool's Prayer

11

Wrestling with angels

"Damn that Falco," Ronnie swore as he recalled his day at the shop and his tussle with the landlord. "He won't get off my back. Now, he's got his lawyer demanding that the rent be paid exactly on the first of the month and you know that increase in taxes from the first of the year? He wants it in one lump sum."

"Can't you get him to accept partial payment?"

"Not this time. Don't you see what he's trying to do? He wants to force us out. Then, he'll rent the place for twice, maybe three times what he's getting from us."

"I get it. We've still got four years to go on our lease. He thought he was so smart when he got us to sign a ten year one. But now, with inflation, it's backfired on him."

"Exactly, and his wife is nagging the shit out of him. She's the greedy one behind all of this. He just does the dirty work."

"But what can we do if he won't accept partial payment? We don't have the cash. Even the amount of money owed to us, if it was all paid up, we would only break even."

"I don't know," Ronnie sighed, his eyes dull with worry. "If I was smart, I'd pull a Chapter Eleven.

"A what?"

"A Chapter Eleven. You know, go bankrupt."

"But that's just what he would like you to do. You've worked too hard, too long." I didn't want him to talk like that. It wasn't the Ronnie I knew and loved. He would never do anything to cheat his customers. "It can't be that bad, yet. Maybe we can get a loan."

"I already have a ninety-day working capital loan."

"How about a personal loan?" I bit my tongue. Why did I suggest that? I detested the thought of it. He would tell the bank he wanted to improve our property and they'd give him a homeowners loan stretched over a three-year period. Our poor house. It needed fixing so badly. But the money always went to pay our creditors.

"I guess that's the only choice we've got."

I knew he was right. "Well, there goes our new kitchen for another three years." Same old merry-go-round. If we could only get out of this financial rut. The business needed a salesman or financial manager or something. But we never had enough money to make the step. Ronnie continued to wear all the hats and do all the jobs and in the printing business it was just too much for one person to handle. Besides, there were more important things to worry about.

"I heard from Lambro about my tests," I said.

"And...?"

"He says I'm okay No ulcers or gall bladder problems or anything. My problem may have been pinworms."

"Pinworms? You're kidding. Even I don't believe that one."

"He thinks I may have picked them up on my trip to Italy."

"I can't believe you have pinworms. That was six years ago."

"Well, I sure don't have them now after all those enemas. Do you think in their enthusiasm they might have accidentally overlooked a few things on the x-rays?"

"I don't think they would do it on purpose. That would be unethical. Let's give them that much credit at least. But they are human. It wouldn't hurt to have them read by an outside party."

"I could call my pediatrician. He might be able to recommend someone around here."

"You know what would really shake them up? Have someone from Cornell Hospital read them, their rivals."

"I bet Wiley would know who to contact."

"You mean, Wiley Coyote? We haven't heard from him in a dog's age. He just faded into the woodwork."

"I guess he's too busy. Lambro also said Tim's next operation is set for the 27th or 28th. They're going to make a new conduit for the urine on his left side and they want to take out both kidneys."

"*Both* kidneys? That sounds too drastic."

"I know."

"The shape he's in now? I don't think he can survive an operation that radical."

"It means he won't be able to put out any urine at all. He'll be 100% dependent upon the machine. You know, he's so proud of the urine his kidneys are still producing. Like he's hoping everything will heal up and get better. A miracle. He wants so much to be normal."

"If the idea is hard for us to accept, imagine what it will be like for him. No kidneys at all!"

"It's frightening but Lambro and the chief surgeon, Dr. Brody, insist it is necessary."

"I think we should talk to these guys. I mean face to face, not over the phone."

"And what's all this going to cost? How are we ever going to afford all of this. There's the rest of the family to think about."

"We'll worry about the cost later. They can't get blood out of a stone."

"I worry about it all the time. It gives me heartburn. My stomach tightens into a knot when I think about it."

"Call Lambro and have him set up a conference with this guy Brody and whoever else is in charge. It's time to lay all the cards on the table. I want to know exactly where we stand and what's going to happen. After all, we still have to sign permission papers for all of this."

"You've never met either one of them, have you?"

"No, and it's about time," Ronnie grumbled.

The pow-wow of the Big Chiefs was held bright and early Friday morning. Dr. Brody and Dr. Lambro faced us across the desk in a tiny office off the main entrance at Wakefield. Dr. Wiesenfeld sat out of the line of fire taking notes inconspicuously. No one passed a peace pipe. The guns were loaded in their favor all the way. Dr. Brody got right to the point.

"Your son has been chosen to take part in our transplantation program. Before we can go ahead, he must have the ilea repaired and his kidneys removed. As you know, the conduit will be made on the left side from a piece of the lower intestine."

Ronnie interrupted. "But do you think Tim can stand such an operation at this time?"

"Yes, we think so," Dr. Brody continued. "In about a month, after everything is healed, he will be ready for the transplant. Dr. Lambro says Mrs. Fringuello's tests look favorable. She is a suitable donor."

Ronnie interrupted again. "Why can't the kidneys be removed in one big operation, the same time the new kidney is transplanted?"

"Because we prefer to do it this way!" Dr. Brody snapped.

"We feel it is a lot safer this way," Dr. Lambro added softening the remark.

Ronnie wouldn't be put down that easily. "We've been observing Tim. He's very weak. He seems disoriented. He can barely walk to the john without getting out of breath. Maybe he won't survive the surgery."

"If we didn't feel he could stand it, we wouldn't do it." Annoyed, Brody raised his voice. "I could go into more medical details but there's no point in it." Sitting Bull had spoken.

I could tell Ronnie was ready to let him have it with both barrels. "There's some other points I want to discuss," I said quickly. I had jotted down some notes so I wouldn't forget. I pulled a large piece of paper from my purse. At the sight of my list, there was a snicker. I looked up to find them all smirking at me. At first I didn't understand the joke but then I realized they were laughing at me. Their low-flung arrows stung my pride and I flushed. Some bedside manner, I thought. Okay you guys, you asked for it.

"About my x-rays. I would like to have a second opinion, someone else to read them."

"What for?" Brody played with the pencil on the desk, still amused.

"Just because I want a second opinion."

"All right, we'll send them across the street," he said brushing me off.

"No, somewhere else, another big hospital."

"Another hospital?" I had struck a nerve.

Lambro butted in. "Let her have them. Let her take them wherever she wants." He knew immediately what I was trying to do. He could see I was ready to go one on one. I looked Lambro straight in the eye and in an instant I knew it didn't really matter any more. His eyes told me he understood and we communicated a mutual trust, a trust that would be unfailing.

"And now about finances. Who is going to pay for all this? We have four other children. My husband is in business for himself. We're barely able to make ends meet. Without my job we'd be in big trouble."

"Well, we've already looked into your hospitalization coverage and it seems to be adequate. In the event it should run out, there are other plans you can apply for. The business office will help you with that," Dr. Brody went on. "As far as bills from us, the doctors, there will be none."

"No bills at all?" I said in disbelief.

"As you know, this is a pilot program sponsored in part by the State. Once you are accepted into the program, the rest is taken care of."

"That's wonderful!" I exclaimed, "but I want it in writing." Shock waves vibrated through the room. My trust in Lambro did not extend itself to include Brody. "This is my greatest concern," I went on. "If I see it in writing I'll be able to rest. My mind will be at ease."

Ronnie said, "When we sign a release for all of this, we're giving you unlimited freedom. You're taking our son and using him as a guinea pig, so to speak. I think we have the right to ask for this in return."

"Without a transplant, your son will die," said Brody figuratively holding a loaded gun to his head.

"Without patients, you'll have no program," said Ronnie calmly.

Brody squirmed. "All right, I'll have my secretary draw up a letter. You'll receive it in a few days."

The conference was over. It was a draw. I wanted to ask Wiesenfeld if he was keeping score. I felt drained and depressed. For the rest of the day I couldn't decide if I should throw up or cry. I needed time to think.

We were afraid for Tim. He was so fragile. Taking out both kidneys left him at their mercy. There would be no turning back once they were gone. Removing his kidneys was symbolic of losing his freedom. Without a new one to take their place we were placing the doctors completely in charge of his body. We were relinquishing him, totally.

It was hard to let go. Especially when the doctors act so superior, so all-knowing, like they were gods. It made me want to rock the boat, to make waves. Like a little kid throwing a temper tantrum when his daddy says 'no' without explaining why. Suppose we refused to give our permission until we got a more thorough explanation? Would it do any good? No, Brody must have his way. Big Daddy could not be questioned. He had the authority. Children obeyed blindly. Naughty ones were punished and refused favors. This was just the beginning of a long association. Harmony was important. Let the Big Chief have his way.

But give us our dignity!

I wonder how others react under these circumstances. Those older than we probably accept the doctor's word as law. But I bet the younger generations, especially those with education, are questioning. They are demanding more rights as individuals. Each one thinks his case is special and he resents being treated like a statistic or a number on a test. When he talks he expects to be listened to and taken seriously. He wants to contribute information that will help his diagnosis and treatment. He knows doctors are human, that they make mistakes and he expects them to own up to the fact they're not infallible, that some of their decisions are based on *their* convenience and not the patient's.

Confidence in medicine may soon be on the same par with politics. Unless medicine can be conducted with mutual trust, the future will be filled with clashes between the medical establishment and the general public. More lawsuits. Right now there are noticeable differences between Brody, who must be about fifteen years older than we are, and Lambro who is much younger. The pedestal upon which the medical profession has placed itself has started to crack. The smart ones, the intuitive ones, are building ladders of trust before it topples. The others are too caught up in tradition, or in making money, or in themselves, to see the world changing around them.

Okay you guys, you've got the drop on us. We'll sign the treaty but you'd better live up to your end of the deal. I'd hate to be the one to break the peace arrow.

On Thursday, July 30th, Tim underwent surgery. It lasted from 9 a.m. to 1:30 p.m. Everything went according to plan. The doctors were happy the way he responded. Tim began what appeared to be a fantastic recovery.

The following Friday, Dr. Lambro called to say Tim was doing so well he could come home after dialysis. It was going to be a big day for us. The girls were coming home, too. Grandpop and Grandma Anderson were driving them up from the shore. It was hard to realize they had been gone for a whole month.

When we went to pick up Tim, I was surprised he was not dressed and waiting. He did not seem eager to leave. We cleaned out the drawers in the night table together. Toys, cards, books and other get well knick-knacks had accumulated and filled several shopping bags. I was concerned when the only pills they gave me were vitamins and amphogel, an antacid. He had been getting shots for pain and I had expected something I could give him 'just in case'.

During the ride home, he complained that the bumps in the road made his stomach hurt. I didn't pay too much attention, thinking some discomfort after an operation was to be expected. It was a happy reunion for all. We barbequed hamburgers, a family favorite, and ate fresh corn on the cob. Tim didn't seem hungry.

That night he couldn't sleep because of 'gas' pains. I worried, maybe I shouldn't have given him corn, it's so hard to digest. They hadn't said anything about diet at the hospital. The next morning, after I came home from food shopping, Tim was still extremely uncomfortable.

"Mom, I don't feel good at all. I got really bad pains in my stomach. You better call Dr. Lambro."

"Okay, Tim. Just take it easy." I knew it must be serious, he seldom complained. I put a call into Dr. Lambro's answering service. While I waited, I felt Tim's forehead. He was burning up. I ran to get the thermometer. 104 °. Not waiting for Lambro, I called Wakefield direct and was told to bring Tim in, immediately. I called Ronnie at work, told Lisa to watch Amy, threw some clothes in a bag for Tim and jumped in the car. Tim was white and drawn, doubled over from the pain.

Dr. Goodman, the resident on duty, examined Tim, took blood cultures and did not seem alarmed that Tim was in pain. Everybody was moving in slow motion except me. No one seemed concerned that he was suffering. The more they dilly-dallied, the more upset I became. I wanted to yell, "Hey, you guys, when Tim says he's in pain, *he's in pain!* Give him a pill, give him a shot, give him something! But no, he was sent for x-rays first.

As I was pushing Tim in his wheel chair to the elevator, we literally ran into Dr. Lambro. *Thank you, God. You answered my prayers.*

"Guess what brought me back to the hospital today, Tim?" The doctor leaned over the wheelchair, kindly. His voice was soothing and comforting. He wheeled Tim down the hall and into his old room. There were no nurses or orderlies around. It was a week-end, of course. The afternoon sun streamed through the high windows. The two of them were silhouetted against the light: Lambro gently lifted Tim in his sustaining arms and lowered him carefully onto the bed. It was as if he was caring for his own child. The sun's rays made a glowing halo around them, a holy vision. The tears in my eyes refracted the beams like prisms as I watched this tender act of love. We had found someone who truly cared. My heart was ready to burst with gratitude to God for this epiphany of reassurance.

The pain was more intense now. Tim's whole body became rigid in repeated waves of convulsions.

"We'll have to operate immediately. There may be an abscess."

It was an interminable period of time before they gave him something to relieve the spasms. If there was only something I could do to help! Finally, the doctors were scrubbed and ready and he was whisked away to O.R.

I stood shaking and alone looking out over the Hudson River as the sun prepared to set. My mind formed a numb, wordless prayer. How could one human being bear such torture? It didn't seem fair. How could God permit this to happen? And under my very eyes? The same old questions and still no answers.

I called home to tell them what was happening. I needed Ronnie now but it was better for him to keep life as normal as possible at home. I would stay and wait.

I remember how Dr. Lambro looked as he walked down the hall after it was all over. He was still wearing the green wrinkled surgical garb and the funny cap and the booties covering his shoes, his red hair in disarray as usual. Exhausted but smiling, the sight of him calmed my fears. He was followed by Dr. Brody.

"Tim's doing fine," Lambro said awkwardly.

"Was there an abscess?" I asked.

"No," he hesitated, "it was peritonitis. There was a leakage from the bowl, the small intestine. Stuff from his stomach was all over the inside of the abdominal cavity."

"Go home and get some rest," said Brody. He almost sounded human.

"I will, I will. I just want to get one good look at Tim to set my mind at ease."

"He'll be out of the operating room shortly. Don't worry. He's going to be alright." They went to change. "Good night."

"Good night and thank you!" How inadequate the words sounded. Before I had been so thankless but now...

I waited another fifteen minutes. As they wheeled out his bed I could see Tim was still under sedation.

"Good night, Tim," I whispered. *Oh God, in this wonderful world of medical miracles, why must anyone have pain?*

The next few days were critical for Tim. He was in intensive care and we could visit him only five minutes out of every hour.

On Monday, he went on dialysis. He couldn't talk because of the tubes down his nose and throat. Around five o'clock Lambro came in.

"Tim looks a little better than yesterday," he said optimistically. It sounded nice but I knew it wasn't true.

"I don't think so. He seems worse to me. Look how he's struggling to breathe. His eyes are not focusing. I think he's lost his fight."

Lambro did not contradict me. "He's tired. We'll sedate him well so he'll sleep tonight."

I waited until he was safely off dialysis and then went home.

The next day Grandma Fringuello and I took turns visiting him in the intensive care unit. He had one tube removed. He was alert but very upset. He couldn't stop the tears from flowing.

"I don't know why I keep crying. It's like I'm so full of water, it just has to come out." He tried to wipe away the tears with the sleeve of his hospital gown.

"That's okay, Tim. You're doing fine." I handed him a tissue. "Don't cry. It will only make your stitches hurt."

Tim sobbed. "I hate it up here. The nurses are so mean. They won't let me have my T.V. They even made the dialysis nurses take out all my get-well cards. I can't have anything."

"What? They won't even let you have cards?" That seemed a bit rigid. Rules are rules, but for a child so young how could they be so cruel? Were there racial overtones to this treatment, also?

"I'm so bored and lonesome. Please stay." He reached out and grasped my hand. It was unusual for Tim to show his feelings.

"They won't let me stay more than five minutes at a time, Tim. But, we'll be back. Grandma is here, too."

Tim started to cry again. "I feel like I'm being punished for something but I don't know what."

"Tim, don't cry." I stroked his head. "Everything is going to be all right."

"Your time is up," the nurse reminded me.

"We have to leave now, Tim, but we'll be back after lunch."

When we came back, Grandma tried to go in but the nurse in charge blocked her way. "There's no visiting now," she said nastily. There were a lot of doctors and nurses milling around inside. She pulled the door shut with a bang.

I went over to another woman who was waiting also.

"Won't they let you in either?"

"No, they're busy with an old man who is dying."

"Oh m'god," Mama exclaimed. "How can they keep a child in

the same room with a person who is dying? Oh m'god. They shouldn't do this. He's too young to be exposed to this." She began to get very emotional.

"Mama, be quiet! You're making a scene." I tried to calm her but there was no use. When I thought about it, what she was saying began to make sense. Knowing the person next to you was dying would not make you feel very cheerful.

"I'm going in there anyway," I said, getting angry. I pulled open the heavy door and went inside.

"I have to see my son," I told the nurse.

"You can't stay in here now," The head nurse practically pushed me out of the room.

"Well, at least let me say goodbye to him."

"Make it quick."

"Tim, we have to go. They won't let us stay. Cheer up. You'll be back in your own room soon."

"I hate it up here," he sobbed.

All the way down in the elevator, Mama, true to her Italian heritage, let her emotions get the best of her.

"We can't leave him up there to watch a man die," she kept repeating, dabbing her eyes with Papa's handkerchief.

What should I do? Lambro wouldn't be around this time of day. Maybe the psychiatrist could help. He would be allowed to visit him. We stopped by his office but the secretary said he was on vacation. Doctors! They're always on vacation when you need them. Who else cared about Tim?

"Mom, you stay here in the lobby. I'm going back up to the third floor, to dialysis. Maybe Miss Plummer can do something."

I went back up but Miss Plummer wasn't there either. I button-holed another nurse, the red haired one that looked about fourteen. She was very sympathetic.

"Why don't you speak to Mrs. Murphy. She's in charge."

"Yes, okay!" As I whirled around there were Dr. Lambro and Dr. Brody, just like in the movies. The heroes arrive in the nick of time.

By now, I had worked myself up into a real case of hysteria. I explained what was happening to Tim, blubbering like a baby. Lambro got the message between gulps. He went right to the phone and called ICU.

"All I can get for you is another ten minutes," he said firmly. "That happens to be one of my best nurses up there. She's having plenty of problems of her own today. I'm sorry, but you will have to go home."

My golden hero had turned into the frog prince. I was humiliated. Holding my head high, I turned on my heels and exited as dramatically as possible. I was so ashamed. Lambro and Brody had seen me lose my cool. I felt like an idiot. Not waiting for the elevator, I fled up the firestairs to the fourth floor.

As I went in, the head nurse sneered, "Five minutes, that's all. I have just medicated him and he is finally asleep. He's been in excruciating pain and won't get any more medication for three or four hours. Don't disturb him."

"I'll decide that," I barked, ready to bite her head off. I went over to Tim and flung the curtain around the bed for privacy. She may have been Lambro's best nurse but to me she was a real bitch. Tim stirred. "What did you do, have a fight?" he asked, his eyelids heavy with drugs.

"Yes, I saw Dr. Lambro and he made them let me in." He smiled contentedly and fell back to sleep. At least he knew I had tried. Of course I wouldn't disturb him. What do they think I am, stupid? She's telling *me* about excruciating pain? Ha!

Even though Tim was sound asleep, I stayed until they made me leave. I calmed down. I was glad the doctors knew there was a problem. All the patients here in ICU were very sick. They needed efficient nursing care. The doctors couldn't afford to anger the nurses, they depended on them. But my son had rights, too. The tension between the Wakefield staff and the dialysis nurses seemed to be building.

The next morning I awoke with a start. I had been dreaming I was standing by Timmy's bed in the hospital. A nurse walked by briskly and said, "All right, get undressed." I asked with surprise, "Who, me?" and she answered. "Yes, the doctor wants to examine you."

I felt so ashamed of the way I had acted the day before. I never wanted to face those people again. I couldn't decide what to do...go to work, go to the hospital or just stay home and hide. Ronnie gave me his advice.

"What can you do at the hospital? Tim will be going on dialysis today. They'll take good care of him. If you stay at home, you'll just mope around. I think you should go to work."

I knew he was right. I didn't feel like working but its drudgery dulled the senses. I would leave work an hour early and go directly into the city.

When I arrived, the dialysis room was busy as usual. Mrs. Murphy stopped to talk to me. She was a little nurse with a big Irish brogue, a little Bantam hen of a woman, full of fight.

"How are you, Mrs. Fringuello," she said kindly, laying her hand on my arm.

"Did you hear about the trouble I had with the post-op nurses yesterday?" thankful I had someone to confess to.

"Oh, those ones," she exclaimed. "Don't let them be a-worrying ye. I hear them 'hiss' as I walk down the hall. There's a wall of ill feeling between them and us. They wish we would just dry up and blow away."

It was good to hear gossip about the hospital. It made me feel it wasn't just me. The slights I noticed were not aimed at just Tim and me but to everyone connected to the program.

"I feel like such a fool, breaking down in front of Dr. Lambro."

"Don't you be worrying yourself about Dr. Lambro, me girl. He admits he's very involved with your son, emotionally. I can see him turn away when Tim is in pain."

My spirits lifted. He was my hero after all. "He really cares about him?"

"That he does. I heard him say repeatedly that he hopes his own children grow up to be as nice as him. If Tim asked for the moon, Dr. Lambro would be the first to try and get it for him."

Fireworks went off in my brain! If she only knew how important those words were to me. I could face anything as long as there was someone on our side.

I went in and sat by Tim. He looked a lot better.

Lambro and Brody arrived. I watched as Lambro came over to talk to Tim. His mannerism was one of concern, his voice remarkably soothing.

I had been planning to give the doctor a peace offering. The first book I had written and illustrated had just arrived at work, hot off the presses.

"Here's something for your kids," I said shyly. "A genuine autographed first edition."

"You illustrated this yourself? he asked, leafing through the pages, "and you wrote it, too?" He acted surprised and pleased.

Tim was wheeled on a stretcher to his old room at the other end of the hall by the dialysis nurse. We were both glad he didn't have to go back to intensive care. The floor nurses suddenly became too busy to help move him into his bed. They acted as if they had never seen him before. Words of contempt were bandied back and forth. The feud seemed ready to erupt.

"To hell with them," the dialysis nurse declared, "I'll do it myself." She was young and tough and not intimidated easily.

I helped her hold the stretcher as she expertly wrapped Tim in a sheet and swung him onto the other bed, all eighty pounds of him.

"There you go, Tim." She covered him with a light blanket. "Snug as a bug in a rug. And if you have any trouble with them," she said, jerking her head toward the nurses station, "let us know down in dialysis."

THE LAST ROUND

Clasp you the God within yourself
And hold it fast;
After all combats shall ye come
To this good fight at last.

God is a mighty wrestler
He battles in the night;
Not till the end shall it be known
What foe you fight.

When God in you is overthrown
He'll show a light
And claim the victor for his own
And crown the fight.

Anna Wickham

12

Act of love

Tim recovered slowly from the peritonitis. The poison seemed to have saturated his whole body. He remained weak and thin. The doctors decided to leave in the tube that drained from the incision. Green pus continued to form in the scar tissue and the wound had to be opened repeatedly to be cleaned out.

Tim's spirits were dampened but he kept on plugging. To cheer him, I sketched a portrait of Dr. Lambro and glued it to a dart board. What better way to take out his frustrations than to throw darts at his adversary?

In spite of everything, Tim entered school in September. Everyone was surprised to see him. On dialysis days, Ronnie would drive him to the hospital by 7 a.m. It was a race between patients as to who would be the first ones on the machines. The feeling was, the sooner you were hooked up, the earlier you would be able to come off. It would take about seven hours for a complete course of treatment.

I was relieved that Ronnie had taken over the transportation responsibility. It was more convenient for him. He was his own boss and had flexible hours. I could count on him. He was the glue that stuck us together during those days. But the strain began to wear on him, also. It showed in his business. Accounts receivable began to slow down. The work was not being turned out fast enough. He lacked enthusiasm to solicit new business.

Now it was my turn to cheer *him* up. The business was his

life and to see it slip through his fingers was as painful for me as it was for him.

We all seemed to be holding our breath. The date for the transplant had been set for October twenty-first, almost on Tim's birthday. I was to start the ball rolling by returning for my final test on the nineteenth, an abdominal arteriogram.

The procedure involved inserting a large needle into an artery in the groin. Through the needle a hollow wire was threaded up to the kidney. All the while I could watch on a T.V. screen. When the wire was in place, dye was injected and pictures taken in rapid-fire sequence. They wanted to make sure this was the right kidney to take. After they were finished, the doctor applied pressure to stop the bleeding for about fifteen minutes and I had to stay in bed for 24 hours.

While I was laying around, Dr. Lambro appeared.

"I hate to tell you this but there has been a change of plans."

"Oh? How were my tests?"

"Your tests are fine, but we need to postpone the transplant."

"But, why?" God give me patience, I prayed silently.

"We can't take the risk. Every time we think Tim's incision is completely healed, we find another pocket of infection. As you know, he must take steroids after the transplant and they will lower his body's resistance to disease. Imagine what would happen if all the bacteria are not destroyed? We could lose the new kidney and everything would have been for naught."

"I understand. It's just I've had my mind set on October twenty-first, all of us have. He's looking forward to getting rid of that inhumane diet, forever."

"Yes, I know."

"Will you tell him? It will sound better coming from you."

"If you want me to."

"When do you think we can try again?"

"December, maybe, or even January."

"That's so far away. I just want to get it over with. I want to get back to living. It's as if the world stopped still, or like living in limbo. This waiting is driving me nuts!!"

I turned my face to the wall. Lambro continued to pace back and forth, running his fingers through his hair.

"We have no choice. We have to wait," he said softly, almost to himself. Then, impatiently, he stalked out of the room.

Up, up and away...run away...fly away...just away. I could think of nothing else. I tried to convince Ronnie to fly with me to Bermuda. As usual his calm logic dissuaded me from my crazy scheme. The fact there was no money brought me back to earth and kept me there.

Tim took the postponement better than I expected. But, when I mentioned it might take place in December over Christmas, he put up a fuss. Even when I suggested he would be able to eat everything, the prospect of being in the hospital over the holidays did not sit well with him. To me, it made no difference this time. Christmas this year was something to be endured, not enjoyed. When the January date was proposed, it suited everyone.

JANUARY 6. Here I was in the same hospital, the same room, but this time I was here for the real thing...the transplant. I was very nervous, my hands perspiring. When anyone spoke to me, I could not control the sarcastic things that came out of my mouth. Everyone knew why I was here and they were curious about how I felt. I wanted to shock them with my witty, irreverent answers and I kept my mind occupied thinking up new ones.

"I feel like getting the hell out of here...I feel like taking a slow boat to China or a fast jet to Tasmania...I feel like cussing everybody out and kicking a waste-basket across the room at the same time...I feel like a cross between the Little Red Hen and Christ in the Garden of Gethsemane...I wish I didn't feel... ANYTHING!!"

Part of the reason I was upset was because Ronnie had not been able to bring me to the hospital. In my anger, I struck out at him, also. Just like the time I was in labor, I mulled, and he drove me up to the hospital steps and said, "Okay, get out," and I did! He drove off while I stood there, contractions coming every four minutes, with my suitcase in my hand. Typical!

But I couldn't complain because Ronnie was delivering a very important printing job to North Carolina. It meant a check for $3,000. He was doing it for us. He was driving all night in the fog to get it there on time. In my frustration I was flailing out blindly at everything and everyone.

An aide brought my food tray. "How do you feel?" she asked. I didn't answer. I peered under the metal cover, suspiciously. As I suspected, a liquid diet.

I had a list of questions I wanted to ask Lambro. So far, no doctors had been around. I had been admitted with relative ease.

Perhaps my complaints about procedure had been heeded, or maybe Lambro was avoiding me on purpose? When Dr. Hunter came in to examine me, I was sure of the latter. He was soft spoken with a gentle bedside manner. In fact, he was so nice I was caught off guard and forgot to ask him anything. They had tricked me again, I thought in my paranoia.

About 3:30 p.m., Dr. Brody showed up. Here was my chance to ask questions. I whipped out my list.

"The anesthesiologist was in to see me and she has me down for a spinal. I thought we had that all straightened out. I don't want a spinal. I want to be completely senseless."

"Oh, yes, you did mention that."

"And another thing, that form we have to sign, it says we will not hold you or the hospital responsible for this or any future operations. As far as I'm concerned there's not going to be any future operations. I refuse to sign it."

Brody bristled. "You'll have to sign or we can't go ahead with the transplant."

"I'll be glad to sign for the transplant, but that's it. Any other operation should be dealt with separately."

"Well, then just cross the other part out. That's what I came to talk about, the transplant," he said gruffly. "We have to postpone it again. For a week."

"What? Not again!" *Oh God, why are you punishing me like this? I'm not a bad person. How much more do you think I can take? I can't stand this waiting, this torture. It's not fair!*

Through clenched teeth I said, "What is it this time?"

"In examining Tim, today, we found a pus-sac like a small boil in the scar tissue. Someone forgot to remove a stitch from the last operation."

My nervousness exploded into anger. "This is getting ridiculous! It's almost laughable, except it's not funny. You're telling me that after all this time some jackass left in a stitch and that the infection will be cleared up in a week?"

"Yes, I'm sure it will be."

"How can you be so sure? Every time you're sure, you end up changing your mind! So what am I suppose to do now?"

"You can take Tim and go home. And try to stay calm. It's rescheduled for next week, the fourteenth. See you then." Brody made a quick exit.

I unclenched my teeth. Go ahead, *leave*, you son-of-a-bitch. And Lambro, you're too chicken-shit to even show your face. In disgust I went out to the pay phone to call home. Ronnie had just arrived back. He was startled when I told him the news.

This time, Tim was upset. "Those jerks, they don't know what they're doing," he grumbled. "Can you imagine, they left a stitch? I wonder how many others they didn't get?" He pulled up his shirt and examined his stomach. The scars looked like the train yard at Grand Central.

"What can we do? If they say wait, we wait."

"I guess there's no use fighting it," Tim agreed with a sigh.

"Did you see the article about us in the Record?" I asked showing him last night's newspaper.

"Yeah, one of the nurses brought it in."

"The information in it is not correct. It sounds as if you need pints and pints of blood. That's one way for the hospital to get donors. The Blood Bank is sure taking advantage of the situation."

Tim studied the article. Then, grinning mischievously, his eyes hinting of the old twinkle, he said, "Now you can't back out."

The postponement was nerve-wracking and embarrassing. Callers were surprised to hear my voice on the phone and I had to explain over and over what had happened. One of the ladies of the church came to the door bearing soup, homemade bread and an inspirational booklet. When she saw me standing there, she almost dropped everything.

Tension mounted between family members. My mother had come to stay with the children while I was in the hospital. All of us crowded under one roof was a strain in itself. Ronnie and I had to bite our tongues more than once as older and younger generations clashed.

I decided to go to work on Friday and Monday even though I felt stupid showing up. I worked like a dog sorting out carton labels. The physical labor wasn't my regular job but it proved good therapy and made me so tired by the end of the day I didn't have any trouble sleeping.

Ronnie was elated because he'd gotten the big check he had been waiting for and was able to pay his taxes. He became more relaxed and that reflected in the moods of the rest of us. My world began to brighten.

The following Tuesday, events proceeded in a more orderly sequence. Just having Ronnie drive me to the hospital bolstered my morale. He helped cut through the red tape of admittance and got me settled. This time I knew it was really going to happen.

Although I was calmer, I still harbored dark feelings of resentment toward all involved. I just couldn't give in gracefully. I still felt I was doing it because there was no other way out. I *had* to do it. I was being manipulated.

In some way I was responsible for my son being in this predicament and it was up to me to get him out of it. As my mother often said, "You made your bed, now sleep in it." This hospital bed of sterilized straw made sleeping difficult, indeed. The feeling of guilt penetrated my every thought. Maybe I was being punished for past sins, for giving birth to an imperfect child, for my selfishness in wanting a career, for creating a work of art. Stop making excuses, you lily-livered, yellow-bellied, chicken-hearted coward, I chided myself.

Later, I had an unexpected visitor, Reverend Bennett. I had never bothered to get acquainted with him because of my spotty church attendance. He was young, still in seminary and lacked the sophistication of a seasoned minister. I was skeptical of his ability to offer spiritual assistance. What could he possibly know of my mental tortures? What could he possibly say to help? I, alone, would be going up to that operating room. Nothing short of a miracle could change that now.

Our small talk was strained. How could I capsulize my fears and apprehensions into five minutes of conversation?

"I worry that Tim will feel I expect him to be grateful. I don't want to burden him for the rest of his life with the feeling of indebtedness," I said trying to find some point to start the conversation.

"We are all indebted to someone at some point in our lives," Reverend Bennett philosophized. It was the superficial answer I had anticipated.

"But this particular brand of indebtedness is cruel, too cruel. It may turn to hate."

Then, he said what seemed to me like a strange statement.

"But, of course, Tim knows you love him."

LOVE? The word ricocheted off the hard green walls and bounced shamelessly around the room. LOVE. I had never considered LOVE. It was too obvious. LOVE. It had a wonderful ring to it. It sounded so right, so natural. Maybe I *was* doing it for the right reasons after all. LOVE. Maybe I did *want* to do it. Dear God, make me want to do it. LOVE rebounded again and again. Yes, yes it's true. *I'm doing this for LOVE!*

Suddenly, I had a terrific urge to tell Tim I loved him. We were a family that never vocalized words of tenderness or affection. Love was a sensitive, vulnerable subject. In Tim's case, love might be mistaken for sympathy and I was afraid of his emotional dependency.

But now, I wanted to say it...before tomorrow. I would chance the consequences. I hurried down to his room. With great difficulty, I struggled to express myself.

"Tim, it looks like it's really going to happen this time."

"Yeah." He seemed to be only half listening but I had to get it all out.

"Look, I just want you to know I'm doing this because *I* want to do it...because I...love you. You never have to say, 'thank you'.

"Once you get the kidney, it's all yours, no strings attached. And if I ever say differently, you can punch me in the mouth, O.K?"

Tim looked up sleepily. "Mom, I know you love me. You don't have to say it. We joke around a lot but I know." He said it so matter-of-factly. He had known all along. It was I who had been so blind. I felt like hugging him. Instead, I squeezed his toe through the blankets. I was satisfied.

"Thanks, Tim. See you in the morning."

That night I couldn't sleep. I didn't want to. There were so many things that needed to be set straight in my mind. All the distorted events began to come into proper focus; my ungrateful-ness to the doctors for their skilled impersonal help, my fear that too much love would turn to sympathy, my selfish struggle for identity, my rebellion against being forced to give. This was not an execution and death but resurrection and birth. My son was being *reborn.*

It was LOVE that made all the difference. I reveled in its ecstasy. Instead of a martyr's cross I had found *the peace that passeth all understanding.*

Call it an awakening, a special message from God, a revela-tion, an epiphany. Whatever it was, it was the most comforting, warm and wonderful sensation I have ever experienced. As I watched daylight push back the night, I was eager for this *act of love* to begin.

See first that you yourself deserve to be a giver, and an instrument of giving.

For in truth it is life that gives unto life...while you, who deem yourself a giver, are but a witness.

And you receivers...and you are all receivers... assume no weight of gratitude, lest you lay a yoke upon yourself and upon him who gives.

Rather rise together with the giver on his gifts as on wings;

For to be overmindful of your debt, is to doubt his generosity who has the free-hearted earth for mother, and God for father.

The Prophet
Kahlil Gibran

13

One glorious moment

The icy water numbed my feet and the sand burned into my back. It had been six months since the transplant operation. I relaxed. We were on the coast of Maine, a land of contrasts.

Sharp, black rock formations, worn into strange shapes by the surf, cradled pockets of white sand. I watched a sea gull circle above the trees that stood perched near the water. At low tide you could walk there but now the waves crashed against the little island, violently.

A voice called down to me from the rock cliff surrounding the cove. I shaded my eyes with my hand and looked into the sun.

"Come on up, Mom," coaxed Tim as he clung precariously to the granite wall.

I waved but didn't budge. I had no intention of exerting myself. The boys looked like frisky mountain goats as they scrambled out of sight. I smiled, trying not to think of the terrible times we had been through. The important thing was, we made it! The operation was a success. Tim had a new kidney, mine, that was functioning well, producing quantities of beautiful urine.

Because the kidney is a foreign substance, Tim's body would continually try to reject it, even though it was a good parent-sibling match. To prevent this from happening, he was taking carefully controlled doses of Imuran and Prednizone, two powerful drugs. There were drawbacks; they lowered the body's resistance to disease, he would need periodic blood tests for the rest of his life, and they were hard on the lining of his stomach. There was also the possibility of other long term effects, such as bone deterioration and even cancer.

As I expected, I recovered quickly from the operation. Since I was healthy to start with, I bounced right back within a couple of weeks. I was happy when they told me the kidney they had taken was big enough to support a football player. It would be more than sufficient for Tim. I felt fine. The only things left were the *scars*.

Had it been worth it? I wiggled my toes under the wet sand and the water rushed in and around the hole. To see him carefree and happy made it worthwhile. What a far cry from the confines of the hospital. How I hated that place. Even the new wing they just completed, I hated. It was shiny new and sparkling clean but depressingly sterile. As soon as you opened those heavy steel doors, the dehumanization began. You became a case number, struggling to preserve your identity, struggling to keep from drowning in a sea of red tape.

During the ordeal, all of us had suffered. Everyone in the family had felt the strain. Tim, in spite of drugs and pain-killers, suffered physical pain, and in addition, there was mental pain, the pain of being manipulated, a pain I had felt most strongly. I was lucky to have someone like Ronnie as my partner. He had supported me through it all. We had changed and grown closer together as a result of it.

The truth is, medicine prolongs *life* but it also prolongs *suffering*. Are we willing or able to accept this truth? We must keep our perspective. Science is but a tool to be used by men, very human men, who find it necessary to manipulate other men in order to reach their goals. Only God can perform miracles. Deciding what is God's will and what is the will of men is the hard part. That's the hell of it. Submission of human dignity to progress is no more acceptable than submission to human bondage.

But that part we could now put behind us. The decisions had been made. The whole family could get back to normal and resume our lives. It was as if we had been sponge diving, holding our breath, and, at long last, we had surfaced to breathe pure, clean air again.

I breathed deeply of the tangy sea air. This camping trip to Acadia National Park was like a pilgrimage to Mecca, a return to a primitive state of existence. We were so starved for nature.

Instead of an adventure, it almost began as a disaster. I had laid out an itinerary but Ronnie wanted to just "jump in the car and go". He forgot that to be vagabonds of the road you should travel light. You shouldn't be driving two vehicles and pulling a trailer loaded with seven kids, our own plus two friends.

We hadn't bargained for the traffic, the heat, or the crowded campsites. Tempers flared and just as I was preparing to sue for divorce, we found a Darwinian paradise off the "stern and rock-bound coast" of Maine.

Invigorated, the girls threw themselves down on the sand beside me.

"It's nice but almost too cold to swim," said Lisa covering herself with a sweatshirt.

"Can we climb up the mountain?" asked Donna.

I rubbed her shivering body with a towel. "After lunch, we'll drive up Mount Cadillac," I said. "The view is supposed to be great!"

It was hard to believe there was a mountain at the seashore. The Jersey coast is so flat. In awe, we drove our van up the steeply winding road. The wind whipped at our clothes and tangled our hair as we looked out over the jagged shore.

"Hey, Leo," yelled Tim over the roar of the wind. "Wouldn't it be great to ride our bikes back down?"

"Wow! Yeah, it sure would," shouted Leo, catching Tim's enthusiasm.

"Now wait a minute, boys, that's too dangerous," I protested in alarm, expecting their father to back me up. I could picture Tim and his bike wrapped around a primeval pine tree. All the worry, time and energy spent on that kid to be thrown away in one glorious moment?! *One glorious moment!* I considered it more carefully. That moment would be the ultimate act of freedom, a symbol of all we had struggled for. Tim was free now of the dialysis machine, the hospital prison. He could do or be anything he wanted just like anyone else. This is what we had been striving for, I thought. This is what it's all about.

Ronnie made no comment. I turned my back deliberately as the boys stealthily slipped their bicycles from the back of the van and cut out down the mountain. In my own mind I was cutting away the ties to the past. I rejoiced in this willful act of independence. The wind stung *my* face as *my* soul glided down the steep stretch of highway with them. I prayed for their safety, thankful that the hand that had guided us thus far would protect them in this joyful expression of life at its fullest. We were celebrating new birth. I had given life to my child twice. Now I was glorifying the rebirth of my faith.

Ronnie called to me, "Do you see what I see?" My eyes followed in the direction he was pointing.

There, shimmering in the far distance against dark clouds, was a rainbow, God's everlasting promise to man.

"But, how can that be? It isn't raining," I gasped in disbelief. As we watched, a second rainbow began to glow above the first in a perfect arc. Ronnie took my hand and together we stood, transfixed. From earth to heaven and back to earth again, God spread his rainbow of miracles and His love.

JOY, SHIPMATE, JOY

Joy, shipmate, joy!
(Pleas'd to my soul at death I cry,)
Our life is closed, our life begins,
The long, long anchorage we leave,
The ship is clear at last, she leaps!
She swiftly courses from the shore,
Joy, shipmate, joy.

Walt Whitman

14

Cry for meaning

"Just what is it you want me to do?" the pastor asked hesitantly.

I gripped the phone tightly. *Dear God, give me patience.* Carefully, I rephrased my request.

"The last time we went through a transplant, I completely ignored the church. That was seven years ago. I was too proud to ask for help. I'm sure I made it harder on myself than it had to be. This time it's going to be different. I'm asking for the church's support.

"The hospital wants to test the whole family to find another donor for Tim. Everyone is to have a blood test. Even Amy, though she's too young to be a donor. It's called a family study.

"Sunday, when we have all the kids together, we'll explain everything to them. If you could be there for moral support, I'd appreciate it. You can act as an objective observer. Maybe you can see something we neglected to see or pick up on vibes we missed. Ronnie and I are so close to it."

"I see," said the voice at the other end of the line. "You're concerned about their reactions?"

"Yes, yes, of course. But, it's more than that. The hospital will tell *me* the results of the tests before anyone else. If I feel for any reason the person shouldn't donate, they will not pursue the matter any further. That makes me the one who decides. They're asking me to play God, in a sense. Do I have the right? Do I have the right to ask one of my children to sacrifice himself for the sake of his brother? They are adults, but just barely. Are they capable of looking into the future, of foreseeing the possible consequences of such an act? Is it fair to place this kind of family pressure on them? These are really heavy questions I'm going to have to find answers to and I want you in on the ground floor so I'll have someone else to share my problems with.

"To sum it up, I want them to know I am in favor of transplantation and yet I don't want them to feel as I did...trapped or forced into it or manipulated. They must have freedom of choice. I want you to act as watchdog."

"So you want me to evaluate the situation?"

"I guess that's what I am trying to say. And to say a few prayers for us."

"Yes, of course," he mumbled.

I hung up the phone. I hoped I had done the right thing. Why did I get the feeling I was the one with the faith and he was the one who needed support?

We gather on Sunday about six o'clock for dinner. Everyone is there. Tim, pale and drawn, weakly takes his place. There is the usual chatter and banter but it is strained. Everyone is aware something important is about to happen. As we are finishing our meal, Reverend Mathews arrives.

"Am I interrupting anything?" he asks cheerfully.

"No, you're just in time. Come in and join us for coffee."

Ronnie clears his throat. "We got you all together so everyone will feel included and we don't leave anyone out. The problem is, as you are well aware, the kidney your mother donated to Tim has been rejected. It lasted seven years which is a pretty good record. The doctors suggest we have the whole family tested to see who else is an eligible donor. I'll be retested, also."

Ronnie signals me to continue. "Just because you are tested does not mean you have to do it. It's not something you can be forced into," I say studying their faces. "If you do it, it's because you want to do it. I don't want you to feel that Daddy or I or the doctors or anyone is putting pressure on you."

"Right," says Ronnie. "If you decide 'no, it's not for me', the matter will be dropped, no questions asked."

"Reverend Mathews is here, in case you're wondering, " I went on, "because I asked him to sit in as sort of a third party. When we went through it the last time, I had no one I felt I could talk to. If any of you feel you want to discuss the problem with someone else other than Dad or I, he is willing to give advice and council."

"To the best of my ability," murmurs the Reverend.

"If you have any medical questions, Dr. Lambro said he will be glad to meet with you or I can tell you about my own experience last time.

"We would like you to give us a little feedback about how you feel concerning all of this. How about a little communication on the subject. Leo, why don't you go first. What is your reaction?"

"Well, I don't mind doing it as long as they take the left one."

"Why the left?"

"That's the side that always gets banged up."

"You mean because you broke your left arm in the motorcycle accident? What's that your unlucky side?"

"Yeah, Do you think it will affect my back muscles?"

"I doubt it, but you can ask Dr. Lambro about that."

"As long as there's pain killers, I'll do it but make it soon."

"How about you, Donna?"

"Well, before I answer how *I* feel, I want to ask Tim a question."

"O.K."

"Tim, do you really want another transplant?"

Tim shrugs. "I don't want to have to stay on dialysis but I don't expect anything from anybody."

"Then, I'll do it. If it will make you look less pale, I mean, wow, you look like the pits right now. Anything is better than watching you stare at T.V. all day. How much can anyone take of the *Gong Show?*"

"A transplant will give him back his old energy," I remark. "Don't forget the old kidney was infected and throwing off poisons. It made him feel lousy."

"Will it interfere with my playing sports, like hockey?" she queried.

"It shouldn't. I can't answer that 'cause I don't play hockey. I'm not into sports," I say facetiously.

Everyone giggles.

"Lisa, you're next."

"What am I supposed to say? Of course I'll do it. He's my brother. How could I ever say 'no'?"

I sense a familiar feeling surfacing.

"What if I want to get married and have children?" Lisa says folding her arms with conviction. "When you did it, all of us had been born already."

"That's true but I don't see why there should be any problems. That's the kind of question for Dr. Lambro. He can answer that one better than I can. And how about you, dear?" I turned to Ronnie.

"Me?" He acted caught off guard.

"Yes, you. Everyone else is saying how they feel. How about you?"

He tries to get out of it but I insist he answer. I know it is hard for him. Like most men, he never reveals his innermost feelings.

He gestures clownishly. "Who does everyone turn to when they need help?"

Lisa leans over and snuggles her head against his shoulder in an exaggerated expression of coyness. "Oh, you Dad." Ronnie beams playing the father image to the hilt. So much for that approach.

"And Amy, they don't want your kidney because it's not big enough yet. It's still growing. So that makes you ineligible."

"Whew!" says Amy leaning back in her chair.

"But they still want to do a blood test on you."

"But, why? I hate blood tests," she whines.

"Because they want to compare the whole family as a group. They even want to take my blood so they can check it against the others."

"There's nothing to it," Ronnie says. "Ask Tim, he'll tell you."

"Yeah, tell me about it," says Tim with a smirk on his face. "I remember a little incident away back when *you* ended up on the floor."

"Oh, that time? I hadn't eaten breakfast, that's all," says Ronnie sheepishly.

The discussion continues as to what day they can all take off to go into the city. I turn to Reverend Mathews.

"What do you think? Did it go well?"

"Even though you are trying hard to present this objectively, I can see the family pressures are there. Each one has said it differently and in his own way. There's really no way to avoid it completely. Sometimes pressure can have a positive reaction. It's a very complicated situation. Let's all hold hands around the table and say a prayer for guidance."

As we clasp hands and bow our heads I think, "What an awful burden to place on them. They're just beginning their lives. It could make them hate being a part of this family, like a curse or a trap. What if one should give a kidney and it is rejected? What a terrible waste! Could they handle it? They are so immature and know nothing about life and its ups and downs. I feel like the war mother who sends her sons off to battle and then watches as they come home, one by one, wounded and maimed. Is there no end to this calamity? *God, help us now as you did in the past. Watch over my children, who are really your children, and give them courage and wisdom to make the right choice.*

We waited for the test results. Leo was impatient, Donna seemed to get flustered more easily than usual, Lisa was nervous and constantly picked on Amy, nagging her like she was her mother.

I tried to keep cool. At times I got that old urge to take off on a vacation to the Caribbean but this time I recognized the call of the Sirens, those mythic Greek sea nymphs whose singing lure unwary travelers, and I resisted. I took a writing course at a nearby university and found it was good therapy. My paper on *spontaneity in art* was well received by my professor, which made me very happy.

In the midst of all this, I had a strange dream. I was with my friend Sue, another teacher, at a school reception held in a private house. The house was sort of old fashioned, Victorian maybe, decorated with very dark wood paneling throughout the small rooms. It was crowded with unfamiliar people except for Mr. Fogel, who is principal of the school where I teach, and his wife. As we passed through one of the rooms I was startled to see my father-in-law, wearing a dark gray suit with vest, his white hair groomed perfectly. This was odd because he has been dead ten years to the month.

He smiled broadly, the picture of health, and reached out to shake hands with Sue. "Hey, how are you," he boomed in that robust voice of his. Then, as he excused himself, I grabbed hold of his hand to show my affection but he pulled away, not rudely but gently. Sue, who knew he was dead, whispered in my ear, "Hey, Judy, you're really something. You can really do it," as if I was responsible for the apparition.

Then it dawned on me that he was the third person we both had seen that day who had been dead for some time. Only I couldn't remember the other two. I seemed to possess an uncanny ability to call up people from the dead. I thought about how good Pop looked compared to when he died and I started to cry, uncontrollably.

I woke up and found myself sobbing in my sleep and told my dream to Ronnie.

A month after the blood tests were taken, we made an appointment with Dr. Brody, Miss Plummer and Dr. Lambro. Ronnie and I walked into the office and there was Lambro with his feet up on the desk, talking on the phone, his hair as unruly as ever. The charisma was still there. I wondered if he was aware of it. It was sort of like an electricity that I felt not so much when I talked to him, but later, a warm glow that shot out across space, a presence, a feeling of perfect security. Maybe it was being on the same wave length. A poet might describe it as a spiritual communion of souls.

We exchanged pleasantries and got down to business; the test results.

"In your whole family the only really good match is Lisa," said Dr. Lambro, addressing the two of us.

"I hoped it would be me," said Ronnie, disappointed for the second time. "It would make things so much simpler."

"Tim predicted it would be her," I interjected, "only I wish it weren't. She's only nineteen. She's going through a very upsetting time in her own life. She's just settling into her new job in a photographic studio. She has a steady boyfriend but they've had their ups and downs. I think the timing is all wrong. She will have a hard time making a decision. I don't ever want to hear her say I pushed her into it. I could never forgive myself."

"It doesn't have to be right away," commented Dr. Brody. "He can stay on the dialysis machine until you think Lisa is ready."

"We can put Tim on the waiting list," added Dr. Lambro. "There's always the possibility he may get a good match from a cadaver."

"Just how good a match is Lisa with Tim?" asked Ronnie.

"*Very* good," said Lambro, emphasizing the 'very'. "In fact, she is almost as good as a twin would be."

"Then my match wasn't that great, was it?" I blurted out, remembering.

"Well, sibling matches always are the best and of course, identical twins are perfect." Lambro seemed to be skirting the question.

"You once told me I was a terrific match...or were you just trying to convince me to do it?"

"Well, for a mother and son match, yours *was* good. I don't regret omitting certain details, especially when it is the mother who will be the donor. They don't usually need convincing."

Aha! I thought to myself, I hadn't imagined the subtle pressures.

"I think we ought to stall the transplant for a while, until she gets her head together," I said making a decision.

"That's fine with us," said Brody. "Tell her she is the compatible one but that she should take her time in coming to a decision. Even if it takes six months to a year."

"When she's ready, she should make an appointment of her own free will and I'll talk to her privately," Dr. Lambro said. "If at any time she hesitates to keep an appointment, we'll take that as an unspoken sign she doesn't want to do it."

"All right, we'll tell her," Ronnie and I agreed.

Dr. Brody said, "For dialysis treatments, we can transfer Tim to a hospital closer to home. It will make commuting easier. Also, Miss Plummer will help him find out about Social Security. Since last time, they've passed some financial bills in legislature that have taken the burden off the patient."

"That's good to hear," said Ronnie.

Again we gathered everyone around the family table. This time the pastor was not present.

"We met with Dr. Lambro," began Ronnie, "and the best donor is Lisa. The rest of us are disqualified for one reason or another. Tim's body, having had one transplant or foreign substance to contend with, has built up antibodies which would immediately reject any of our kidneys. I don't understand why but because of these antibodies, fewer kidneys will be right for him, even from cadavers. Tim is lucky that Lisa shares a certain combination of genes with him that the rest of us don't have."

"I knew it would be Lisa," said Tim confidently.

Lisa nodded. "So did I. Hey, does that mean you won't make me pay any more rent money?" she said slyly.

Leo and Amy were quiet but Donna said, "You know, I had a dream that it was Lisa. But she didn't want to do it and Mommy kept insisting. Then, Lisa and I had a fight, a tug-a-war over something, only I can't figure out what it was."

"Probably, Lisa's kidney," I interjected.

"Now, we'll never hear the end of it. It will be my kidney this, my kidney that. I'm the best one and yours isn't." Donna imitated their childish arguments. "Mom, don't let her do it. I can't take it." She jumped up from the table and stalked off. We continued the discussion, ignoring her outburst.

"Dr. Lambro thinks we should wait a while before the operation, say six months or so," Ronnie continued. "Tim, you've adjusted fairly well to dialysis so you'll continue, three days a week, only you will be able to go to a hospital nearby instead of all the way to New York. This will give Lisa time to think it over and decide if she really wants to do it."

Tim looked at his father with surprise but Lisa was pleased. "That's good," she said. "Then I can arrange to take off from work before vacation and it will give me extra time to recuperate."

"I would like you to talk to Dr. Lambro," I said earnestly. "You remember him don't you? You met him once before."

"Yes, I remember him. But, I don't want him to go into any gory details or explanation about machines or anything."

"No, it won't be like that. It's more to answer any questions you might have and to see if you've got your head on straight. If you set up an appointment and then change your mind, that's okay too. You can back out any time you want. Also, you'll have to have tests like I did to make sure you're healthy."

Lisa pushed back her chair from the table.

"Okay, but I want to talk it over with Dave."

"Yes, he should be included in whatever decision you make."

We were alone and I said to Ronnie, "I feel like we should get her a medical alert tag to wear around her neck. Suppose she's in a car accident or something."

"Don't be silly," said Ronnie. "That would only bring more attention to the problem and make her worry about herself more. Besides, we are trying to avoid having her feel like the fatted pig waiting for slaughter."

"You're right. I wouldn't be surprised if she backs out. It's a tough decision to make."

"We can make it easier for her if we drop the subject and wait for her to bring it up again herself."

Another example of Ronnie's common sense.

It is Good Friday and I reflect upon the Crucifixion. Christ suffered once on the cross but my son suffers daily. I wonder how he can stand the pain of the needles on dialysis, the ordeal of submitting himself to treatment. It's not the big hurts so much as the small ones that add up and make life impossible to live. What courage if takes and what effort! "He's adjusting nicely" is a farcical phrase. Adjust...or die. Adjust...or go crazy. It's easier to adjust when there is hope but what if hope should be cut off? I wonder if deep down inside each "well-adjusted" person on dialysis there isn't a dark, secret place that is as bitter as a spring tonic, an indescribable hatred for life. Someday, Tim may wake up and say, "Okay! That's it! I'm through adjusting," and quit.

But, there I go looking only at the pessimistic side. Every

Good Friday has a resurrection, an Easter morning. I must look through this morbid tunnel of faithlessness and into the joyous light. Tim has been spared death all these years. God must have some wondrous plan for him. I must have faith even though His plan has not been revealed to us. Perhaps, it never will be.

Spring drifted into summer and I hardly felt the transition. Half-forgotten memories of seven years ago dragged down my senses and my brain refused to function. It was spring then, too. I had no energy to work in the garden as we waited to hear who would be the donor. I didn't cry now as I did then but a terrible feeling of sadness saturated my being. Funny how life seemed to be replaying itself. Like a rerun of an old movie, one I never wanted to see in the first place.

One day, Donna told me about a mini-course she was taking in high school about death.

"I don't know if I believe in a hereafter, a heaven," she said, not realizing Tim was sitting in the next room, listening.

"Well, Donna," he piped up sarcastically, "why do you go to church if you don't believe?"

Donna was startled and then began to defend herself and at the same time attack his seeming lack of values.

"Hey, how can you talk when you never go to church?" she said vehemently. "You don't believe in anything. What are you doing with your life? You're just vegetating."

Tim fought back more aggressively than either of us expected. "How do you know what I believe? You don't know me! I bet you'd be surprised to know I haven't missed saying my prayers at night for the past four years."

The verbal sparring started to get out of hand. They cursed at each other and called names. I finally got them separated. I was shocked that Donna was so intolerant but at the same time elated that Tim was able to express himself with so much feeling. The encounter, while unpleasant, was good for both of them and relieved built up tensions. At least I now knew he believed in God. He needed to trust someone or something. I said a prayer of thanksgiving and asked for His grace on us all.

THE HIDDEN JEWEL

My child, the empty slate
Upon whose breast
World's wisdom will be etched,
Rubs out my faint scribblings, crying
I press too hard.

How can he know
The chalk of life
Is as hard as marble dust or that
Fate's hand does not render
Tender strokes?

Sadly, I mourn for him,
My tears salted with
Bitter-sweet memories of adolescence;
My child is dead! A stranger
Resentfully stares back.

Oh, Rock of Ages,
How long must I wait for you
To chip away stone walls of discontent
And find a precious jewel of love
Hid within his heart.

J. Fringuello

15

A saint 9 ain't

The headlines of an article in the local evening newspaper caught my eye, *Politics and Payment of Kidney Dialysis*, with a subhead: *Taxpayers may have $1 billion burden in 1980*. My interest was piqued and I kept on reading.

> *...Home dialysis is also cheaper. Medicare pays $147 per treatment in a hospital or clinic-about twice the cost of the same treatment at home.*
>
> *Yet despite the advantages and lower cost, only about 10 to 15 percent of all kidney patients do their dialysis at home. The rest go to hospitals or clinics running up bills which could cost taxpayers an estimated billion by 1980, say Medicare officials.*
>
> *Dr. Belding Scribner of Seattle, a pioneer in the use of artificial kidneys, says the government could save $150 million a year if more patients were on home care.*
>
> *Noting that 60 percent of the patient population could do their dialysis safely at home, Scribner says there is an overriding reason why most patients go to the hospital: it costs them less...*

The article was accompanied by a picture of a girl and her mother sitting relaxed in their own living room with the dialysis machine in the background.

My blood pressure rose instantly. Nowhere was there any

mention of transplantation. If all the patients were transplanted, there would be no need for machines. How one sided, I thought. They always picture dialysis as so easy. Just plug yourself in and *presto* you're cured. If they only knew the true story.

I stewed inwardly forming mental rebuttals to the slanted information. The public should hear the truth, the suffering that accompanies the miracles, I decided as I began to set down my thoughts in a letter to the editor. It was my responsibility to tell the truth as I saw it.

Editor, The Record:

The cozy picture of Dorothy Harris and her mother in the article, "Politics and Payment of Kidney Dialysis," May 25; makes dialysis at home seem relaxing and even inviting. Let us look for a moment beyond the first impression.

The funny-looking machine in the background controls Dorothy's entire life. Without it she would die within a short time of uremic poisoning. Her blood is being pumped through one tube into the machine and out the other continually for about five hours.

The process of filtering is simple. The machine must function perfectly and everything must be sterile and clean. The tubes are inserted into a vein in the patient's arm, leg or groin by two giant needles. Painful? Of course! The vein is able to take this abnormal treatment because it has been sewed together with an artery in a previous 'minor' operation. The artery pumps the blood into the vein, enlarging it and keeping it from collapsing temporarily.

Dorothy's mother looks relaxed but she is not. She must constantly monitor the machine and the patient. She must take Dorothy's blood pressure at intervals and test her blood to make sure the impurities are being removed.

If the machine is pumping too fast, the patient may become nauseated and experience a burning sensation. If it is too slow, it will not be efficient and more hours are necessary. Mrs. Harris is a courageous woman to shoulder this responsibility. I hope she does not have a large family or younger children who demand her attention.

Kidney patients are constantly anemic. Frequently they need injections of iron and vitamin supplements. They are more susceptible to colds and other diseases. Their lungs can become filled with fluid, making breathing difficult. High blood pressure, retention of fluids in the tissues and other side effects are frequent. It may be easy to train someone to run the machine but will a lay person without nursing background be able to interpret danger signals before it is too late?

Dorothy is fortunate she has a house big enough to contain this dialysis machine. She's lucky to have room to sterilize and store the equipment, that there is sufficient electrical and water supply. Tell me, Mrs Harris, what do you do in a blackout? Can the machine be repaired immediately? Can you get spare parts? And how does one resolve the guilt if something does go wrong? (Even doctors don't operate on their own families, I'm told.)

People who depend on kidney machines live on hope, hope that tomorrow or the next day they will get a new kidney, a transplanted kidney. I know because my 21 year old son has that hope. Most don't consider dialysis a permanent situation. If they did they would go insane, commit suicide, or become a vegetable.

Where can they get a new kidney? From a living family member if there is one available and their tissues match. Or from a cadaver. The number of patients on the waiting list far outweighs the number of kidneys available.

Taxpayers object to paying billions of dollars for kidney dialysis and patients object to having to depend on a machine for life. The obvious alternative is not for more machines but for more transplants.

People, ignorant of the facts, refuse to talk or think about transplants. For some strange reason they think they will need their body after death. They are too grief-stricken when a loved one dies to sign a release to allow the kidneys of the deceased to be used. Movies like "Coma" make them even more suspicious.

Kidneys are wasted every day because hospitals and ambulance corps are not alerted or equipped to preserve cadaver kidneys. And government intervention may tread on religious beliefs, a touchy situation. Your newspaper could help, not by one article but by continually advertising the need for donors, by educating the uninformed.

As a living donor, I would like to suggest to all critics, that instead of paying $1 billion in 1980, each donate one healthy kidney to a person on a dialysis machine in 1978. Recycle your body, today!

The reaction to the article was as if I had knocked over a hornet's nest. A letter answering mine appeared in the Voice of the People column a week later from outraged members of the dialysis staff at the hospital. They said I was painting a bleak and disturbing picture of dialysis, that patients do adjust, that they and their dialysis partner are adequately trained and that my statement, that patients might "go insane, commit suicide or become vegetables" had no validity.

A few days later, another letter was printed, this one from Mrs. Harris. She felt sorry for my bitterness and would pray for me.

So they think I'm a pessimist, do they? Well, they've completely missed my point. I'm not attacking dialysis. After all, it's saving my son's life. I'm debating the critics of dialysis, the ones who are so money-conscious. I object to scare tactics from them and from the slanted headlines of newspapers. I want the lawmakers who control government spending to be aware of the whole story. We've come a long way with financial aid and we wouldn't want to lose it, nor would I want to be forced into doing home dialysis just to save a buck. That is what I fear most of all. I was willing to give a kidney so that my son wouldn't have to go on dialysis. That's how strongly I felt and still feel about it. For some, home dialysis may be the answer but patients and their families should have a choice. I'm fed up with rose-colored pictures of the wonders of dialysis, any kind, home or hospital.

When I got home from vacation there was a letter waiting for me. An invitation from the nursing supervisor at the hospital, Mrs. Thompson, to attend a Patient Information class.

I brushed it aside, thoughtlessly, until Tim said, "Everyone in dialysis read your article in the newspaper."

"Oh, really? What did they say about it?"

"They think you're over-reacting."

I snickered to myself, wondering why they were all so concerned about one person's opinion.

In a few days there was a call from the social worker at the hospital, Mrs. Peters.

"Mrs. Fringuello, I am new to the dialysis staff and I'm trying to get to know all the patients and their families."

"Yes?" I was overwhelmed by their concern.

"Could you come down to the center next week or if you can't make it, I'll come to your home."

"Well...alright. I'll be down next Tuesday about 2 p.m."

Tuesday came and I was nervous. I asked Ronnie to come with me but he had to work. Marisa, my sister-in-law, was busy, too. I persuaded Donna to accompany me, not just for moral support but as a sounding board. I wanted another set of ears.

We arrived around two and Mrs. Peters introduced me to Anne Thompson, the supervisor who wrote me the letter.

I agreed to attend the Patient Information classes next week.

Mrs. Peters began to question me about the family. She was a heavy-set woman in her late fifties.

"Tim has how many brothers and sisters?"

"Four, two and two. Have you talked to Tim yet?"

"Ummm, yes, but he's very well-defended, as young people are today."

"Defended? What do you mean, 'defended'?"

"You know, guarded in his feelings."

"Yes, that's true. It's hard to communicate with him."

"And is this one of your daughters?"

"This is Donna. She's eighteen. Her sister, Lisa, is twenty. She's the one who has been tested as a possible kidney donor for Tim."

"Oh, they don't like to take another donor from the same family, especially a young female."

I was taken aback by her conviction. I wondered where she got her information.

"I don't think you should make a statement like that. The doctors in New York think she is a perfect donor. If I had had any doubts about letting my daughter do it, you would have just reinforced them. I think you are stepping out of bounds."

She was silent for a minute. "Maybe you're right. I take back what I said."

The damage has been done, lady, I think.

"What is the policy here about transplantation. Are they for or against it?" I queried.

"I'm really too new to know. I used to be a psychiatric social worker for cardiac patients at another hospital. There's so much to learn about dialysis," said Mrs. Peters.

"It's just I heard rumors they don't look too favorably on transplantation. They discourage them."

"I don't think that is true. There seems to be a goodly number of cases in the file cabinet who have been transplanted."

"How do you feel about it personally?" I asked, putting her on the spot.

"I'm for it. But I definitely think you should talk to someone more qualified. Dr. Jenkinson can answer your questions better than I. If he's too busy today, I'll make an appointment for you. Oh, here he is now. Doctor, this is Mrs. Fringuello. She'd like to ask you a few questions."

"How do you do. Yes, I can see her in a few minutes." he said as he brushed by.

As we waited I was surprised at how calm I felt. I reminded myself to be pleasant and non-aggressive. Doctor Jenkinson ushered us into his personal office, not spectacular but well appointed, several comfortable orange, fake-leather chairs, an executive-size desk.

The doctor was of average height and build, slightly balding on top. A mustache, closely cropped beard and even white teeth reminded me of Sigmund Freud. His stylish, dark-framed glasses made him look serious. He wore a white clinic jacket buttoned by the top button only so that his flowered tie could be seen above and below it. All through the interview I had the almost uncontrollable urge to unbutton it and straighten his jacket.

"Your son, Tim, is one of our dialysis patients I understand," he began smoothly. "And you're the mother of ten children?"

"Ten! Please, do I look that bad? No, only five," I chuckled nervously.

"Well, I don't know, my cousin has ten and she looks terrific. And look at Ethel Kennedy."

Yeah, I think, and look at her money, but I just smiled promising myself I wouldn't be the first to start anything.

Taking my newspaper article from a drawer, he laid it on the desk in front of him. "I read your letter to the editor and I wanted to talk to you about it, personally You're off base with many of the statements you made," he said getting to the heart of the meeting.

"That's very possible," I said in a self-composed manner, "as it is based strictly upon my own experience which I know is limited."

"Where did you get your experience?" he retorted.

"Where Tim was transplanted in New York...Wakefield."

"Compared to our operation, Wakefield is very small. They do not have the staff we have. They are not as well equipped. Do you realize, that the same director back in 1963 didn't believe in transplantation *or* dialysis? He thought it was better to let them die."

"Really?" I said, refusing to be shocked. I reached into my pocketbook and took out a small black notebook and pen. "What would you say is the average length of time one can expect to live on a dialysis machine?"

Jenkinson cleared his throat. "It is very hard to make generalizations. It's very individual. It depends upon the age of the patient, his condition, if there are any complications such as diabetes, cardiac disease and so on. About 13% die each year. But when you look at the elderly age of many, it is not surprising."

I was writing feverishly in my notebook. He eyed me suspiciously.

"Uh, may I ask why you are taking notes? Are you planning to write another article?"

"I like to keep a record of statistics. I pick them up wherever I can find them. I've kept a daily journal since Tim was very small."

A flash of annoyance passed between the doctor and Mrs. Peters.

"What you stated in your article about patients not adjusting to dialysis is not true. If you walk through the clinic you can see for yourself. They are very happy."

"I know of a seventeen year old boy who was Tim's roommate at the hospital. He took an overdose of drugs. It was considered a suicide," I countered.

"That's just one isolated incident."

"We also know of a lady on dialysis in New York City who refused to come for treatment unless they picked her up in an ambulance. Isn't that a little maladjusted?"

"Anyone who has a serious disease, no matter what it is, must adjust and accept treatment. If they don't the other alternative is rather permanent."

"But you are ignoring the fact that there *is* an alternative. Transplantation. I think you are grossly misinterpreting my letter," I said, deciding to take the offensive. "I'm not saying dialysis is wrong. I'm sure there are many who adjust. I wanted the public to know all the facts, from all angles. It's unfair to put the blame for high taxes on the patient. Don't you agree with me that the newspaper was using sensationalism to attract attention? Such publicity may influence Congress to pass laws requiring all patients to be dialyzed at home."

"That's not possible," said Jenkinson. "Congress started out pushing for a law that would require 50% of dialysis patients to be treated at home. Then they dropped it down to 40%, then 20% and finally they took it out altogether. I would never permit a newspaper to print anything derogatory to discourage patients on dialysis in any way. For instance, I would never print that 50% of them will be dead in five years."

"You mean you never tell your patents that?"

"Well, if they ask me point blank, of course, I'll tell them. It would be unethical not to tell them. I just wouldn't publish it or make it general knowledge. I have one patient who has lasted thirteen years. The odds are getting better. If everyone got transplants, it wouldn't help the taxpayer either. You know how expensive they are."

"They don't have to be. Especially if they become more routine. I still insist you have missed the point I was trying to make. What were those statistics again, 50% in five years?" My pen was poised.

"Weren't you listening? See that, you can't even get your facts straight here. Your problem is, you're a specialized reader. You only read what you want to hear."

My heart beat faster. A heat wave crept over me. Keep calm and ignore the slurs, I told myself. "Well, there are two doctors who thought it was a good letter."

"Who, Brody?"

"Dr. Lambro for one."

"Who? Lambro, oh, he's a urologist." He said it as if he had inserted the word "only". My smile remained frozen.

"He was second in command at the time of the transplant. He's a surgeon," I said, defending my hero.

"But he's a urologist. They can be surgeons too, you know."

"I don't know his exact title but he agreed with me."

"What did he say?"

"That the answer probably lies somewhere in-between, that the patient should have a choice."

"Well, I agree with that!"

"And so do I. That's why I am concerned that Washington might pass some law that would limit the patient's choice, that would make home dialysis mandatory."

Jenkinson patted my article and said, "I don't want you to think we are adversaries, or enemies. I want us to be friends." He rose and extended his hand.

We shook hands gingerly. I was satisfied that he had not succeeded in intimidating me. He had not pressured me into changing my mind. But I was still puzzled as to why everyone was so concerned about my opinion. What were they afraid of?

It was Monday morning and I arrived at the hospital for the

Patient Information classes. Again, I brought along moral support. This time my friend Sue, a former nurse and now a teacher. She knew several of the nursing staff but not Mrs. Thompson.

There were several other patients attending. One young man was married and had a two-year-old son. He had chosen dialysis over transplantation. What a waste! Another couple in their fifties were training for home dialysis. The woman would be running the machine for her husband. She was nervous but determined. I admired her courage. A young patient brought her mother who would be her partner. They attended one class and then dropped out. Some were not yet patients but expected to be as their kidneys ceased to function.

Mrs. Thompson addressed me after class. "Thank you for coming, Mrs. Fringuello. What does Tim think about you attending classes?"

"I don't think he is really aware of it. I told him but it didn't sink in. I really don't see that much of him, maybe an hour at supper."

As classes proceeded, we got numerous hand-outs and scientific explanations of the body, the kidneys, the bladder and so forth. I wondered if she gave a test at the end? We discussed the emotions of a person suffering from uremic poisoning, how they fluctuate from one extreme to the other.

"How does Tim get along with his peer group?" she asked singling me out.

"He gets along fine with them. He has a group of friends that he goes biking with. He has a Harley Davidson. It's just *me* he doesn't communicate with."

Uh, oh. I shouldn't have said that. Now she'll get the impression there is an abnormal gap between us. There is a gap, that's true, but most 21-year-old males don't discuss their friends or their social life with their mothers. Leo never does.

"Maybe you should take more time to listen," she said going into detail about her experience with her own daughter. "I took her on a shopping trip and gave her the opportunity to have me all to herself. Then, she would open up and tell me what's troubling her."

"I don't think it would work with Tim. He'd think I was nuts if I asked him to go shopping."

"Well, that's just an example. You must try in some way to make more time for him," she councils wisely.

Yeah, sure lady, I think. Maybe if I could tie him down for five minutes.

The two weeks are up. As I was about to leave, Mrs.

Thompson intercepted me. She was anxious to hear how I enjoyed the class.

"I always find I am better expressing myself in writing than talking face to face," I said.

"Then, by all means, write it down. I would like very much to know your reactions."

And so would Jenkinson, I muse to myself. "Okay." I hand her a letter I had written the night before. "It's all in here."

> *I am pleased that Timothy is in the hands of such dedicated and sincere people. Because you care, there is an atmosphere of loving concern in the dialysis department which is felt by everyone involved.*
>
> *Mrs. Thompson, you did an excellent job of simplifying a complex subject. In evaluation I would like to make one constructive comment. Although your teaching approach is perfectly acceptable, perhaps, you might consider a less conventional one. Most people are there because this whole idea of kidney dialysis is new to them. They have fears and questions about the procedure itself. Perhaps the first class and even the second should have had more discussion about the machine itself. A room set up with chairs in a circle would help the flow of conversation and we could get to know each other better.*
>
> *I know you were there to present facts not clinical procedure or conduct a psychological rap session. But it was hard for me and I am sure the others, to look at it strictly from that point of view without constantly thinking how it related to my situation. I am thinking also of Tim. If he were to attend he might not come back after the first class unless he felt more involved.*
>
> *Now that the course is over, I have taken out all the articles that were in the newspaper and read them again. I was surprised to find my article remarkably accurate. In spite of what Dr. Jenkinson says, all the questions I raise, while I now know the answers, are very real problems. In fact the class has reinforced my fears because the basis for them is true. The only thing I would change is to add, "While there are those who do adjust, there are those who do not."*
>
> *Perhaps it was the tone of the article that upset everyone. It was deliberately written that way to attract*

attention. It was the sensationalism of the other news arti-
cle in reverse. The original was meant to scare taxpayers
and I wanted to show the more shocking side of dialysis
that most people are unaware of. I get annoyed at those
who make dialysis sound so easy and trivial, like the
answer to everything.

I am a very optimistic person and so is a Tim. I knew
that the first transplant would be a success. It gave Tim
seven years of an almost normal life. Would he be in the
condition he is now if he had been on dialysis all that
time? I don't think so.

I am not against dialysis. How could I be? It has saved
and is saving his life. But in my estimation a person is
cheating himself if he doesn't go for the whole ball of wax.
There is an unquenchable desire in everyone to be normal,
to be whole. Especially someone Tim's age. The dialysis
way of life means settling for something less than normal.
True, you can adjust and will when the alternative is
death but who really wants to? Or more importantly,
should *you want to?*

Transplantation is far from perfect. I have some very big
doubts in that department, also. Those doubts go all the
way back to "does man have the right to play
God?" Sometimes I even think Tim should have been left
alone at the age of five. Think of all the heartache, the
expense, the hours that have gone into saving that little
body. If I was a pessimist or bitter I would be writing
about that. But the dominate side of me keeps insisting,
yes, it has been worth it. If not for him directly, for some-
one else through his experience.

I think as medical people, working so close to it for so
long, you have become nearsighted. Sympathetic but not
empathetic. For a moment, put yourself in this situation:

One day I say to you, "From now on for twenty hours a
week, in order to save your son's life, you must set aside your
medical profession and paint his portrait."

"But, I'm not an artist. I have no talent," you say.

"That's okay You can learn."

"But I can't stand the sight of paint...it's so messy."

"That's okay You'll get use to it."

"Suppose I make a mistake while I'm painting?"

"You can't make mistakes. You must paint it perfectly."

"Wouldn't it be better if you painted it? You're so much better than me. It's your profession, while mine is medicine."

"Yes, but you can't afford me. You'll have to do it yourself."

"For how long will I have to do this?" you ask, starting to panic.

"No one knows." comes the answer.

The person who accepts the responsibility for dialysis on a loved one is an unselfish, unsung hero.

I conclude that...a saint, I ain't...

A few days later Mrs. Thompson answered my letter with the following:

Thank you for your letter, I read every word at least three times. I also read your article.

There is no way I can tell you I know how you feel, you alone know that. I can only tell you that each patient here is a part of my life. I am concerned about them, their families, and the effect caring for them has on my nursing staff.

Like you, there are many nights sleep is hard to come by - I toss, worrying about who will supply the care the patient needs at home, when there is no one home to care, or what can I do to make my staff nurse know how important she is to the patient.

There are times when I wish I were rich enough to give them three times their salary - and then I realize - it is not the salary that keeps them in dialysis nursing - it is something I had little to do with - it is that inner quality of caring and loving. I thank God for them and finally sleep comes.

Thank you, Judy, for coming to class. If you need our help please let us know. All of us are here because of patients like Tim.

Saints do walk on earth, Judy...

Seven months passed. I was getting uneasy. Lisa had not mentioned meeting with Dr. Lambro.

Should I prod her a little? Ronnie and I met with the

Reverend for advice.

"Do we have the right to nudge Lisa a little?"

"I have found from experience that even though children come of age according to the calendar, they still wish and seek parental guidance," said Reverend Mathews. We, as parents, have the right and duty to guide."

"Then, you don't think it would be pushing to encourage her to make a positive step?"

"On the contrary. Perhaps, she is waiting for you to suggest it."

"Then, I'm going to start leaving Dr. Lambro's phone number in obvious places. Maybe she'll take the hint."

The hints went unheeded. Finally, I confronted Lisa. "Have you thought about making an appointment with Dr. Lambro to discuss the transplant?"

"No."

"You really should. By the time everything is straightened out, it will be the first of the year." I handed her the doctor's address and phone number.

"I don't know what to say to him. What shall I talk about?" she said, sensitive to my meddling.

"Don't worry, he'll know what to say to you. I think you ought to take Dave with you."

I answered the phone the next day and it was Dr. Lambro.

"I'm returning Lisa's call," he said.

"She *did* call?" I said, relieved. "She's still at work. I hope you do most of the talking because she's a little nervous about meeting with you."

"We'll make out just fine. How's Tim doing?"

"Pretty good. It's just he never tells me anything. Now that he's getting Social Security he seems to have the attitude, 'Why should I work?' It's like he's on an extended vacation."

"It takes time to adjust to a new way of life. Be patient with him," Lambro said.

"He eats just about everything he feels like eating, even salty things."

"If the treatments are going well, his diet is not so crucial. It used to be, but the machines are much more efficient. Stop worrying. I'll call back later." Lambro hung up the phone.

Lisa and Dave returned from the appointment.

"We almost missed Dr. Lambro," said Lisa flippantly, "cause we were late."

I turned away from my typewriter. "How did he impress you?"

I was curious if she noticed the same charisma.

"He was awfully fidgety. He made it sound very simple, no big deal. He said I should tell Tim I can do it between such-and-such-a dates and make him decide if he wants to do it or not. I told him, 'My mother wants him to do it' and he said, 'Your mother should stay out of it. It's not her decision'." Lisa looked at me for my reaction.

When there was none, she continued, "He thinks the whole thing was handled wrong from the beginning. Everyone should have been asked, 'who wants to donate' and only those who volunteered should have been tested. And I shouldn't have been told it was a perfect match."

Now he tells me this? We were following their suggestions. We thought we were being so careful.

"We didn't say you were a perfect match. You assumed that because we said yours was better than mine."

Lisa continued, "He admits he puts more pressure on parents because he feels they owe it to their kids."

My hero's golden halo had begun to tarnish.

Lisa and I cornered Tim at the dinner table.

As usual, Tim was grumpy and reluctant to talk.

"Well, what about this transplant business, do you still want to do it?" I said getting down to the nitty-gritty.

"Not right now," said Tim. "I'm sick of the hospital."

"I can't say that I blame you. Three times a week is a lot, but transplantation would change all that." There was a sinking feeling in my stomach. Had someone from the dialysis department at the hospital talked him out of it?

Lisa said, "Yeah, you better make up your mind. I'm not going to stick around forever."

"Tim," I pleaded persuasively, "you have to figure a transplant is going to extend your life even if it lasts only seven years. Lisa's kidney might last even longer."

"This is living?" Tim snickered sarcastically.

"Well, I just want you to know, you can have my kidney," Lisa said. *At last she said it,* I thought to myself. She had made up her mind. *Thank you, God.*

"Nah, I don't want it," Tim mumbled, trying to walk away.

I was shocked. "You don't want Lisa's or you don't want any kidney?" I asked, hoping to pinpoint his true feelings. "You can still be on the waiting list for a cadaver."

Tim turned and faced the two of us. In a firm voice he said, "If I was going to do it, I wouldn't want a cadaver. I'd take Lisa's because she's an almost perfect match. The chances of rejection would be less. I don't want to put it in...take it out...all that hassle.

"And, I don't want to do it at all! With a kidney I would have to hook up to a tube and bottle at night like I used to do. Then, I'd have a urine bag to worry about during the day. I'd have to empty it, sometimes it would leak, sometimes it would smell. Now there is no urine at all, no bag, no fuss. Dialysis is the lesser of two evils."

"Well, if you change your mind..." said Lisa, feeling repulsed.

"Maybe, in a couple of years...*no*, I don't think so." Tim had made his decision.

"Well, according to Dr. Lambro, there are a lot of things being invented that are making dialysis better," I said, trying to hide my disappointment.

"Yeah, that's what I keep hoping."

Yes, we must keep hoping...and praying.

Saint, *n. a dead sinner revised and edited.*

Ambrose Bierce
from
The Devil's Dictionary

16

Final chapter

At 3 p.m. on February 10, 1995, at the age of 38, Timothy James Fringuello died. Actually, now that I think about it, he died hours earlier - his spirit, that is. But his body refused to give up as a whole team of hospital personnel worked on him feverishly.

It was sudden but not unexpected. I felt it was an answer to my prayers because if he had become an invalid, it would have been the final insult to his identity as a human being. The last hours left an indelible impression upon me as well as his sister, Donna, who played an important part in the final drama.

For the last couple of years, Tim had been getting progressively weaker. He weighed a little over 100 pounds. His five-foot two-inch frame was skin and bones under his clothes. Never a quitter, he tried to build up his frail physique by a daily regime of weight lifting and step aerobics to improve his joints. He watched cooking shows hoping to put on some weight through nutrition. He was always interested in what I was planning for dinner and he even learned to make some of his favorite dishes and treats.

Although he couldn't hold a normal job, he was forever busy around the house with one project after another. One summer, he built an eight foot fence. He would construct a section flat on the ground and then enlist his father's help to lift it into place. In fact, he did so much construction that the local lumber yard gave him a discount, thinking he was a independent contractor.

He convinced us to tear down the old oversized garage which

was taking up space and inhabited by rats and squirrels. He almost single-handedly erected a smaller, more compact tool shed. Whenever he needed help with the heavy work his father, his brother or his friend John would give him a hand. When it was finished, I had a hand-carved sign made with the inscription, "Tim's Place" for his birthday. But he never would hang it up. He said it made him think of *Mr. Roger's Neighborhood.* I had been thinking more along the lines of a place like *Cheers.*

This past winter he'd spent working on our new kitchen. He did the planning and the construction down to the fine details. He worked with an urgency, from early morning till late afternoon. He could barely hold a hammer because of a condition called "trigger finger". His knees were as stiff as a man twice his age. But he kept plugging, never complaining. And now, I have a beautiful kitchen. In fact, everywhere I look in the house I see evidence of his handiwork. "It's going to be just you, now," I chided my husband.

"Yeah, I know," Ronnie admitted sadly. "He's going to be a hard act to follow."

The Sunday before his death, we had a wonderful family celebration. Our daughter, Donna, was visiting with her husband, Vincent, and their children, Chloe´ and Candice. They live in Paris and flew over to have baby Candice christened in our church. It was a joyful reunion of siblings and their families, aunts, uncles and cousins. Tim, though quiet, enjoyed the day. Donna was scheduled to return to France on Saturday.

Friday night was to be a big night for me. Our annual "Meet the Artists" art show sponsored by Pascack Art Association, of which I was president, was to be held at a local restaurant. I had promised to bake a couple of cakes which would be served along with other home-made desserts after the buffet.

As I passed his door to go downstairs that morning, I saw Tim sitting on the edge of his bed looking miserable. I knew he had a cold so I said, "Are you all right? You don't look so good. If you don't feel like driving, I'll take you to dialysis later."

Tim grunted a little which I took to mean "Yes". He continued to sit there sort of huddled over, rocking slightly with his hands clasped between his knees. He looked like a wizened old man.

I proceeded downstairs and spent an hour or so baking. As I started upstairs to get dressed, I heard Tim's voice. I thought he was calling to me. I rushed up to find him stretched out on the bed, moaning. His every breath was labored. I realized something was drastically wrong. I quickly called down to Donna and Vincent, who were preparing breakfast.

"I need help! I think there is something wrong with Tim!"

Donna and Vincent rushed upstairs. I was trying to hold him up to open the passageway for his breathing. I thought maybe some phlegm from his cold was blocking his lungs. Donna ran to call 911 and then came back to try her skill at mouth-to-mouth resuscitation. He didn't respond. Finally, after what seemed like an eternity, the ambulance arrived. After repeated attempts at resuscitation the paramedics decided his sugar was low and gave him an injection. Tim immediately opened his eyes and looked around dazed.

"What happened?" he mumbled. We tried to explain he was having some kind of seizure and that they were going to take him to the hospital. As they bundled him up in the sheet for transportation, he kept crying, eerily, "Help me God" over and over.

There are several turns down our staircase and they had a difficult time maneuvering him.

I said, "And he only weighs 100 pounds. Can you imagine what a time you would have if it were me?"

One of the attendants looked over his shoulder and quipped, "Well, if you feel sick, be sure to come down stairs." I knew he was trying to keep things light in view of the circumstances but I didn't feel like laughing.

They asked if I wanted to go in the ambulance but I wasn't dressed. I was accustomed to the hurry-up-and-wait techniques of hospital emergency rooms, so I opted to drive myself. I called Ronnie, dressed quickly, then, packed a few things I knew Tim would need and left for the hospital.

An emergency room can be a frustrating place. Tim was in excruciating pain but no one could do anything about it until his doctor gave the okay. X-rays and tests had to be taken to be sure they were treating the right problem.

Tim's feet and hands were cold and tingly. There seemed to be no circulation. I tried to rub his feet. His stomach hurt ...and his back. He was having trouble breathing.

I asked the nurse to get me something to wipe the white froth from his lips. She brought a packet of wet Q-tips with a lemon flavor. He seemed to appreciate it. I asked for a pillow to put under his knees as he kept drawing them up in pain but none could be found. Finally, the nurse rolled up a few sheets and tucked them under his legs. I asked if it helped any but he was so engulfed in pain he didn't respond. Nothing we did seemed to help.

By now everyone connected with dialysis had heard that Tim was in the emergency room They came down one by one to see if it was true. The social worker tried to comfort us both. She was upset. Tim seemed to be a favorite patient in the dialysis unit.

A male nurse came to take him for a CAT-scan. He tried to get him to drink some horrible mixture. "What, are you crazy? Can't you see he can't drink anything? He'll probably choke," I insisted.

Then, finally, they brought him back. I stroked Tim's head as the doctor gave him an injection of sodium bicarbonate to make him breath easier. But the solution burned, a freezing burn and Tim complained loudly.

An intern came to take some blood. He was having difficulty and I asked, "Are you having a hard time finding a vein?"

Baffled, he replied, "His blood pressure is so low I can't even find an artery!"

He kept prodding him mercilessly with the needle. Some blood started to seep into the vial. Tim, all of a sudden stopped his writhing and became calm. His eyes glazed over. He stared straight up at the ceiling in a catatonic stare.

I was frightened and gasped. "There's something wrong. Tim...Tim, what is it?"

The intern immediately stopped what he was doing and called for help. He slapped his face gently and said, "Tim, don't leave us!"

But...he was gone. His pain was too overwhelming and he finally gave up the fight. At that moment, I believe, Tim's soul flew away to meet Jesus.

I was asked to step back as a team of doctors and nurses took over. His systems seemed to be shutting down one by one. As they revived one, another shut down. They worked continually for the next three hours.

Ronnie arrived with Donna and baby Candice. I was thankful they were here. "I think, maybe, *it is his time*," I said, hardly daring to speak the thought.

They rushed Tim up to ICU. We were asked to wait in a room nearby. Time slipped by. Ronnie was restless. He wandered over to see if there was any word. He returned with the news that Tim had had a heart attack but they had revived him. Ronnie tried to get me to go for a walk. He meant well but I could not stir from the spot just in case Tim needed me.

Amy called on the phone. We describe the situation to her. Her nursing experience was very helpful. She said if there looked like there was no hope tell them *DNR... do not resuscitate.*

Ronnie squeezed my arm. We called the doctor out and told him the dreaded words...*do not resuscitate.*

Like magic the room that had been full of people began to empty out. Donna and I entered. "We've been through so much together," I sighed, kissing Tim on the forehead. "We love you, Tim."

The nurse was watching the monitor and in less than three minutes she announced that it was *flat line.* "Tim is gone," she said matter-of factly.

The tears came. We all spent a few minutes alone with him. The pain was over. Tim was at peace, at last.

As the message spread about Tim, I became aware that he had led a secret life away from home. At least it was secret from me.

I knew that every Monday, Wednesday and Friday at 10:30 a.m. he would drive himself to the hospital, hook himself up to the dialysis machine, eat his lunch which included a grape soda and, then, when he was finished about 2:30 p.m., he would drive himself home. I could set my watch by him. He was in the self-help unit which meant he did a lot of the treatment himself with a minimum of supervision. My fears of home dialysis never materialized, thank God. He had been on dialysis for almost eighteen years.

What I didn't realize was how much Tim was loved and respected at the hospital. He went about his business in a no-nonsense way, never complaining unless there was something really wrong, pleasant and friendly, setting an example for the other patients.

When one of the reclining chairs broke that the patients use during treatment, he became concerned that nothing was being done to replace it. He made a big sign saying "GARBAGE" and pushed it out of the dialysis unit. He wanted patients to be as comfortable as possible.

He death was taken to heart by everyone who knew him there. His loss was everyone's loss. It was like a little family in the unit. A couple of workers became so upset that they requested to be transferred to another department. His stable presence would be missed by all.

I always felt that because he had experienced so many miracles in his life he should take up the standard and become an activist for some kidney-related cause. I believed because his life had been spared he should do something purposeful, like make speeches or organize support groups...something to make his life have meaning. What I didn't realize was he was actually accomplishing more by his example than all the speeches he ever could have made. His calm presence, his patient acceptance of his fate made him an unsung hero in the eyes of all those who crossed his path.

To attest to this, I received an insightful letter from the hospital chaplain written the night after Tim's death.

A Reflection

It is now 12:15 a.m., and I sit with tears rolling down my cheeks as I reflect on the day just completed.

"Hi, how are you today? You've got a new "do" - it looks good!"
The young man who spoke those words to me had eyes that danced with the light of the Lord, and a smile that always touched my heart. A deep gentleness always emanated from Tim; I always felt so privileged to bring to him the Body of the Lord, and Tim was always so grateful. As I placed the Sacred Host in Tim's hands that day, and looked into his eyes, I remember praying that Tim would truly know how precious he was to the Lord Jesus.

The above encounter took place a week ago; This afternoon at 3:00 p.m. our beloved Tim accepted the full embrace of the Lord and gently went home with Him. Tim's last hours were caught up in all the life saving efforts of a team of very caring health care workers, while his family struggled in the decision making process which would most respect Tim's wishes for a death with dignity.

I had never met Tim's family, yet our shared love for Tim eased the meeting under these circumstances. I felt one with his Mom, Judy, his Dad, Ronnie, and his sister, Donna, who was then nursing her new daughter, Candice. I could feel their pain in their "Letting go" process, and held each one in my heart.

While Tim's family members-Mom, Dad and sister Donna went in to be with Tim for his dying moments, I was privileged to hold his precious niece. As she lay

*sleeping on my bosom, I whispered into her ear that
she would always have the love of her so special Uncle
Tim. I told her not to be afraid as she sensed the sadness now, for it was a sign of just how much her family
members loved each other, and that everyone would be
okay because of the love they shared. I told her that
her Uncle Tim would always be watching over her,
because he would always love her, and that one day
they would get to really play in the presence of God.
As Candice slept in my arms, Tim went home.*

*Later, after his family left, I went in to say my good-
bye to Tim. He looked so peaceful, like a child sleeping
securely in the arms of his mother.*

*I will miss Tim's dancing eyes and ready, gentle
smile. I am so grateful for the privilege of sharing in
his journey of faith in the midst of great suffering.*

*Thank you, Lord for sharing your precious Tim with
so many of us...*

Another life I knew about only vaguely was the one he led
with his peers. All through high school and for a long time after,
he rode his Harley Davidson with a group of guys on weekend
excursions up-state, down to the shore. They were a motley crew
with black leather jackets and reflection sun glasses. When they
partied, he was always the designated driver since he couldn't
drink. When he graduated from high school, he celebrated with
the others by getting a tattoo on his upper arm with the embell-
ished word, *Freedom.* I was aghast, of course, like any mother,
but there was more for me to worry about. An infection might
have caused his kidney to reject. But Tim was exerting his man-
hood in this right of passage.

As time went on the group began to fall apart, some moving
away, some getting married. His best buddy, Greg, finally took
the plunge. Even though Tim knew and liked Terri, Greg's fiance´,
he was very shaken up. I could sense his bitterness over this
'betrayal' of friendship. He must have felt completely abandoned.
My heart ached for him.

When they had their first baby, a boy, they named him
Timothy. I was thankful that they continued to include Tim in
their plans. I would scold him for not making an effort to keep up
their friendship. When I mentioned my concern to Terri and
thanked her for still seeing Tim, she acted surprised. "I guess you

don't know Tim," she said wisely. "He's a great guy. We'd never think of doing anything without him."

Tim finally gave up his bike when he became too weak to pick it up.

As his friends gathered at the wake they still looked to me to be a little on the wild side. Those big, hairy, bearded men, wearing leather jackets with Harley Davidson insignia, stood with tears coursing down their cheeks. Some placed photos of Tim on his bike in the casket. They knew a different side of his personality that Tim had kept hidden from me or that I had refused to acknowledge. For them, his death was the equivalent of losing their own carefree adolescence.

At the funeral, his friend from high school days, Fred Canavan, read a touching memorial to Tim.

...Timmy was many things to many people - all good, never evil - energetic musician, enthusiastic biker, careful carpenter, gentle fishkeeper, magnanimous friend. Though he was meek, his capacity to endure adversity without complaint made him a giant among us.

I hear his music...his drums ring and I hear a cadence to which all our hearts can march. I feel the thunder of his hammer reminding us to build and rebuild our ties to our families and our friends. I can never forget his friendship when I see the reflection of a gentle man in the easy ripples of his garden pond.

So as we carry Timmy's remains to his place of rest, we will be strong, we will not strain, we will show no sign of burden. He will not be heavy, he is our brother...

I will remember all these things and
cherish them in my heart.

THE BLADES OF GRASS

In Heaven,
Some little blades of grass
Stood before God.
"What did you do?"
Then all save one of the little blades
Began eagerly to relate
The merits of their lives.
This one stayed a small way behind,
Ashamed.

Presently, God said,
"What did you do?"
The little blade answered, "Oh, my Lord,
Memory is bitter to me,
For, if I did good deeds,
I know not of them."
Then God, in all his splendor,
Arose from his throne.
"Oh, best little blade of grass!" he said.

Stephen Crane

Epilogue

It has been a few years since Tim passed away. Today I visited his grave. The snow has finally melted and I can see a few green sprouts shooting up. I had planted grass seed last fall but this looks more like weeds.

We managed to get Tim's headstone up in time for his birthday in October. It is quite handsome, a dark gray granite veined with white. The family came and the minister said a few words of consecration. Then, we had a luncheon together complete with cake and candles. I know Tim would have liked that. We all miss him.

We had a wonderful family get-together at our house on Christmas, also. It was wild and noisy and a little crazy what with nine grandchildren running around. But it's a holiday we won't soon forget.

I've managed to keep busy. I'm a member of the choir at our church which has helped a lot. It's hard for me to be depressed when I sing. Pascack Art Association has kept me going, too. There's always meetings and exhibitions and bus trips to organize. I really haven't felt like painting. It's funny because when the kids were little I couldn't wait to have some time to do my artwork. And of course, there was this book I promised myself to complete.

Ronnie has been working his head off as usual despite a few medical set backs. The only way I can get him to take a day off is to go somewhere special. I guess it's his way of handling grief. He finally finished installing the tiles for the back-splash under the kitchen cabinets. If Tim had been here, it would have been done months ago.

What a beautiful day this has been, the sky bright blue, the birds singing. Spring must be just around the corner. I think I'll get a little birdhouse and hang it on the tree near Tim's grave.

Words to a song keep running through my head...

This is the day that the Lord has made.
Let us rejoice and be glad in it.

Bibliography

Page 11	William James, *The Will to Believe*, Dover Publications
Page 77	Henry James, *The Ambassadors*, Charles Scribner's Sons
Page 87	Hippocrates, *Law, bk I*, Harvard University Press
Page 127	Edward Rowland Sill, *A Fool's Prayer, Bartlett's Familiar Quotations*, Little, Brown, & Company
Page 143	Anna Wickham, *The Writings of Anna Wickham*, Salem House Publishers
Page 153	Kahlil Gibran, *The Prophet*, Alfred A. Knopf, Inc
Page 161	Walt Whitman, *I Hear America Singing*, Delacorte Press
Page 191	Ambrose Bierce, *The Devil's Dictionary*, Oxford University Press
Page 203	Stephen Crane, *The Collected Poems of Stephen Crane*, Alfred A. Knopf, Inc.

ORDER FORM

Please send me____copies of the book,
Tim's Place by Judith I. Fringuello
I am enclosing $_____
$17.90 ($12.95 + 4.95 for shipping and handling)
plus 6% Sales Tax for NJ Residents ($.78)
I understand I may return this book for a full refund, for any reason.

LIMITED TIME OFFER TO FUND RAISING GROUPS
Purchase 50 or more books at $10 per book and we will
ship free of charge. Sales tax where applicable.

SEND TO:

Name_____

Address_____

City_____State_____Zip_____

Telephone (____)_____
E-mail_____

Please send order form and check to:

NU LEAF PUBLISHING
P.O.Box 77
Emerson, NJ 07630

Fax: (201) 262-7285
E-mail: ArtJIF @ aol.com

ORDER FORM

Please send me____copies of the book,
Tim's Place by Judith I. Fringuello
I am enclosing $_____
$17.90 ($12.95 + 4.95 for shipping and handling)
plus 6% Sales Tax for NJ Residents ($.78)
I understand I may return this book for a full refund, for any reason.

LIMITED TIME OFFER TO FUND RAISING GROUPS
Purchase 50 or more books at $10 per book and we will
ship free of charge. Sales tax where applicable.

SEND TO:

Name_____

Address_____

City_____State_____Zip_____

Telephone (____)_____
E-mail_____

Please send order form and check to:

NU LEAF PUBLISHING
P.O.Box 77
Emerson, NJ 07630

Fax: (201) 262-7285
E-mail: ArtJIF @ aol.com